WB   LYN

D1143196

x

Guns Along the Canyon

Only one man believed there was gold in Riva Canyon. He was proved right and the rush started as did the killings. Then the local ranchers became involved as their water supply was polluted and their cattle put at risk. Unless drastic action was taken it would all explode into a range war.

It was down to Marshal Dave Anders to keep the peace, but what could he do? He was faced with shootings, explosions and mysterious disappearances that sent him off to Mexico in search of information. His life was in danger there, and when he got back home, things had worsened with the threat of a lynching.

Once again the marshal had to make tracks to the border, for only then could peace be restored. But could he survive the violence?

Guns Along the Canyon

TOM BENSON

A Black Horse Western

ROBERT HALE · LONDON

© Tom Benson 2002
First published in Great Britain 2002

ISBN 0 7090 7101 9

Robert Hale Limited
Clerkenwell House
Clerkenwell Green
London EC1R 0HT

Typeset by
Derek Doyle & Associates, Liverpool.
Printed and bound in Great Britain by
Antony Rowe Limited, Wiltshire.

ONE

The woman was thin but strong-looking, with a tanned face that might have heralded any age between forty and sixty. Her firm mouth was a thin line as she drove the lightly-sprung rig into Halo Township. Although covered in trail dust, there was a neatness in her dress that could not be hidden, and her greying hair was pulled back in a tight bun held in place by a large comb that was almost like that used to support a mantilla.

She drew rein half-way down the dusty main street and the quiet bay gelding nodded its head as if in agreement with the welcome pause. The woman looked around, observing the saloon over on the right, the various food stores, the lawyer's office, and the only hotel with its large, gilded sign. She could see a forge and feed-store at the far end of the street next to some corrals, and there was a schoolhouse adjacent to a white wooden church that had its door tightly shut.

It was a quiet town, with just a few people on the street, and they seemed to be too apathetic to take any interest in the stranger. She sucked at her thin lips as if to clear the dust away, and then urged the animal on a few more yards until she came level with the marshal's office. It was a building made of brick. The only one that stood out in its newness. She stopped the animal there and climbed down from the rig. After tethering the horse to the hitching rail, she mounted the two wooden steps and entered the domain of the local lawman.

Marshal Dave Anders was young, tall, and with broad shoulders below an impassive, almost Indian face. His hair was fair, rather long, and matched the pale eyebrows above deep grey eyes. He was cleaning a shotgun when the woman entered and put the barrel down on the desk as he rose to greet her.

'Good morning, ma'am,' he said in a cheerful voice. 'You sure look like you've travelled some. Take a seat and I'll pour you a cup of coffee.'

'That would be a kindness, Marshal,' the woman said as she pulled the bentwood chair nearer to the desk and lowered herself wearily into it. 'I've come from Tucson, and it's one long way to drive a wagon at my time of life.'

The marshal paused in the act of pouring the hot liquid into large mugs.

'That's some journey, ma'am,' he said with admiration. 'And may I enquire as to what brings you here?'

'My husband. I'm lookin' for him.'

The marshal's mouth tautened a little. 'Well, I don't know as that's quite my line of country, ma'am. Chasin' after husbands that have run out. . .'

'He ain't run out, bless you, Marshal. He's workin' somewhere around here and this is the nearest town he mentioned in his letters. But I ain't heard a blame word for two months or more. He always wrote regular. Posted a letter on the stage every couple of weeks, and then – nothin' all of a sudden.'

The marshal handed over the coffee and went back to sit behind the desk.

'What would be his name, ma'am?' he asked as she sipped the hot drink.

'Bill Conyers.'

Dave Anders relaxed a little and permitted himself a slight smile.

'The prospector?' he asked.

'That's the fella. You know where he is?'

'Sure do, ma'am, and don't fret too much about gettin' no letters. The stage ain't been through as regular as usual. There's been heavy rain on the route and a few landslides. I don't figure as how you have anythin' to worry about. Bill Conyers ain't come to no harm.'

The woman took a deep breath as though some heavy weight had been lifted from her shoulders.

'I'm right glad to have that news, Marshal,' she said thankfully. 'Can you tell me where to reach him?'

Dave Anders got up and went across to point to a rough map on the jailhouse wall. It was a hand-made thing with trails and creeks depicted in various coloured crayons. Ma Conyers joined him to peer at it with short-sighted eyes.

'He's here at Riva Canyon.' The marshal put his finger on the spot. 'It's about fifteen miles from Halo Township and almost due north of here. The trail's easy to follow because it was once a big gold-mining area. Everybody worked there at one time. Twenty years ago that would be. Your man is the only one out there now. There ain't no gold.'

'He says different.'

'I know, and he's been workin' there for months now. Comes into town now and then for supplies, but he never brings in any dust or nuggets. I guess he's just living in hope. They tell me he's even staked claims back in Tucson. All legal-like. But the folks in this town don't take him too serious.'

She permitted herself a tight smile. 'I know. They laugh at him,' she said. 'He told me so in one of his letters. But Bill figures to prove them all wrong.'

Dave Anders nodded. 'I'm afraid that's true, ma'am. We all know around here that the gold is

8

worked out. This was a boom town when I was a kid. Now, it's just what you see. A little place that's goin' nowhere in particular.'

The woman took the cup from her lips and looked hard at the young lawman.

'My Bill is an experienced prospector,' she said firmly. 'He says there's gold in that canyon, and I believe him.'

'Has he found any?'

She shook her head reluctantly. 'Not yet,' she admitted, 'but he's sure that all the signs are there.'

'Well, I hope for your sake that he's right, ma'am, but the locals are certain sure that the whole place was worked out years ago.' The marshal shook his head sadly. 'This town would certainly start bustlin' if there really was gold out there. We'd be a real busy place again.'

They had both sat down as they talked while Ma Conyers finished her coffee and thanked the lawman for his aid. He gave her detailed directions to the canyon, made out a copy of the map on a sheet of paper, and escorted her to the door of the jailhouse. She would stay in town overnight at the Austin House hotel and go look for her husband the next day.

Marshal Anders thought no more about the eccentric gold-hunter in the canyon. He had two missing horses to find and a report of a cattle raid by some

9

drunken Mexicans from below the border. It was nearly ten in the evening of the following day when he returned wearily to Halo Township after wasting several hours tracking down the cattle rustlers only to find that the animals had merely strayed into a gulch and stayed there near the cool stream that ran through it. The horses were still missing and there was nothing much he could do about them.

There was a rig outside the jailhouse and he heaved a sigh of annoyance when he recognized the bay gelding that waited patiently at the hitching rail. Ma Conyers was back, sitting on his porch and rocking slowly back and forth in his old chair. Her face was in shadow but there was something in her posture that filled him with foreboding.

'Evening, ma'am,' he said as cheerfully as he could while he hitched his own horse to the rail and loosened its girth. 'How can I help you?'

'I'm not sure as anybody can help me any more, Marshal,' she said in a broken voice. 'My Bill is dead.'

The lawman ushered her into the office and sat the stricken woman down on a chair while he lit the oil-lamps and put a vesta to the kindling in the stove. Neither of them spoke while he placed the coffee-pot above the flames and ladled in the crushed beans. It was only when he had laid out the mugs ready for the drinks, that he sat down behind the desk and faced her.

10

'You'd better tell me all about it, Ma,' he said in a sympathetic voice.

'There ain't a great deal to tell,' she murmured sadly. 'He's been dead a long time by the looks of it. Eaten by coyotes and buzzards; just a skeleton now. I don't know how I'll break the news to my boy. He's near to twenty, but ain't quite growed up, as you might say. He'll take his pa's death real badly.'

The marshal leaned across the desk. 'Is he – have you left the body there?' he asked gently.

'Sure did,' she said, 'but I reckon we gotta give him a proper Christian burial. It's the least we can do. My Bill was a good, hard-workin' fella. Have you got a mortician in this town and a preacher who can say a few words?'

'Yes, ma'am, we've got all that. I'll do everything that needs doin' first thing in the morning. I don't reckon you have any idea as to how he died, have you?'

'Couldn't rightly tell.' She thought about it while the lawman poured the coffee. 'All his stuff is still there, and his gun is in its holster. There's no sign of any trouble that I could see. He was just lyin' there by the edge of the water as though he'd been panning. The pan was still there with dirt in it. Maybe he was took by heart trouble. He was older than me by a few years. Nigh on sixty, he was.'

'Could be, ma'am. I seen fellas drop awful quick

11

like that. And it can be mighty hot in Riva Canyon.'

A little group gathered outside the marshal's office the next morning. The mortician was sitting on his flat wagon with his assistant at his side. Ma Conyers was aboard her own rig, and the marshal was climbing into the saddle of his roan mare ready to lead the way to Riva Canyon. The sun was warm and threatening to get hotter. The only consolation was a steady breeze that blew almost horizontally across their path. It carried a fine dust that dried the mouth and made the eyes ache with its grittiness.

They made slow progress out of Halo Township and along the well-defined trail to the north. The marshal led the way to keep out of the dust cloud that was raised by the wagons. He was cursing the long ride when he really needed to take some rest after the efforts of the previous day. At the same time, he felt great sympathy for Ma Conyers and showed it by his every action.

The mortician took a different view. This was a business trip for him and he was enjoying it. Pete Weldon was a tall, thin man with a face perfectly suited to his craft. Being miserable came second nature to him and he drove his mules with funereal dignity. His coat was black, as was the cotton stock around his neck, and he wore black cotton gloves that matched the length of black cloth that was wrapped around his tall hat.

It was a solemn procession that stopped for a break after a couple of hours and resumed when the animals and people had eaten and drunk. The mortician's assistant took over the driving of their flat wagon. He was also in black, but young and shorter of stature than his boss. He had an open, rather stupid, face, and nobody at first glance would have realized that the two men were father and son.

They at length reached Riva Canyon. It loomed ahead like a dark gash in the reddish cliffs that threw deep shadows in the afternoon sun. The canyon had a wide mouth with plenty of bushes and small trees growing around it. It tapered as it cut like a writhing snake into the hills and fizzled out to a mass of scree that climbed towards dark strands of taller trees up near the sunny peaks. A stream ran down the middle of the canyon. It was clear and fast, and the horses and mules raised their tired heads at the smell of the water. The stream broadened as it left the shade of the sloping walls and veered west to flow out over the grassy plain. The hills from which it came were like some black smears on the horizon.

The little party moved slowly into the echoing mouth between the cliffs with Ma Conyers now in the van as her little rig clattered across the uneven ground, cutting through the meandering creek as she led them to where her husband lay dead.

13

It was a peaceful-looking scene. The stream ran strong and a couple of feet deep at this point. There were old spoil heaps around, showing earth and gravel of different colours with tufts of grass sprouting between them. The noise of the water was loud, and in the sloping walls of the canyon, tunnels lay shadowed where miners had once dug for gold.

A rough tent of dun-coloured canvas was erected in the lee of some overhanging rocks. A dead cooking fire was in front of it with coffee-pot and skillets lying nearby. A shotgun was leaning against a ridge of sandstone while blankets lay folded near it, warming in the dry air.

There was no sign of a man at first. Ma Conyers had to stop her rig and dismount to lead the way some twenty yards further on where the canyon narrowed and most of its base was taken over by the noisily flowing creek. She turned to the men who were following her and pointed with a thin finger.

The skeleton lay on the bank of the stream with water lapping at its head. The clothes were gone but one leather boot was still there and a gunbelt with a holstered pistol encircled the waist of discoloured bone. There was a greasy hat nearby and an old tin watch on a silver chain was lying among the ribs.

'The coyotes have sure been busy here,' the

14

mortician said with a certain morbid relish. 'And them buzzards has had their share, I reckon.'

He nodded towards the birds that sat high above their heads or circled the canyon, looking for more food.

'I wonder how he died.' It was the marshal who spoke as he kneeled at the side of the skeleton and carefully lifted the watch from among the bones. He passed it to Ma Conyers and she tucked it into a pocket beneath her skirt. He unbuckled the gunbelt and passed that over as well.

Ma Conyers took out the Colt and checked its load. 'He sure didn't shoot at nobody,' she said sadly. 'Is his poke there?'

The marshal shook his head. 'No sign of one,' he said as he ran his hand among the sand and gravel.

The woman stirred uneasily. 'It has to be somewhere,' she said. 'I made that for him myself and he never let it out of his sight. Any cash money he had would be in that poke, Marshal. And any gold dust he found. My Bill wouldn't go losin' that.'

'It ain't here, ma'am.'

The mortician had helped his son to get the light wooden casket off their flat wagon. It now lay alongside the skeleton as he waited for the marshal to move away and let him get on with his job.

'No ribs smashed,' Dave Anders said as he examined the bones carefully. 'And no other breaks anywhere. I reckon he did just die of a heart seizure, ma'am.'

He stood up and motioned to the mortician to take over. The tall man and his son began to move the bones carefully and pack them into the wooden box. It was when the skull was lifted that Pete Weldon suddenly let out a long, unprofessional whistle.

'Well, one thing's for sure,' he said as he held it up for inspection, 'any heart seizure he had was caused by a large piece of lead.'

Dave Anders looked at the back of the dead man's skull. Somebody had put a neat bullet-hole there.

TWO

It took them more than an hour to clear the site and load everything onto the rigs. The skeleton of Bill Conyers was treated with as much reverence as possible as it was laid to rest on the back of Pete Weldon's wagon. He and his son then helped to gather up the cooking utensils, spades, bedding, and tent, to pack them all away in Ma Conyers' small rig.

The mortician emptied out the prospector's pan, flinging the dried gravel back into the stream and rinsing it before placing the thing on top of a roll of bedding.

They had found the fatal bullet. It rattled around in the skull and eventually dropped out when the mortician shook it violently. Dave Anders pocketed the piece of lead and made a final search of the area before they set off again for home.

Their arrival back in Halo Township caused little stir and even the funeral on the following morning was hardly enough to generate a ripple of interest among the local people. Dave Anders attended, and so did the mayor. But it was all over very quickly and Ma Conyers left town to return to Tucson just after noon. Only the marshal watched her go and noted the sad droop of her shoulders and the lost expression in her eyes.

He returned to his office in a thoughtful frame of mind and hardly took any notice of Pete Weldon leaving town with his son at his side on the rig.

The town mortician was a shrewd business man. Pete had been apprenticed to the trade as a youngster and had always made a good living out of the dead. His father had also been a mortician and had always told him that the service was one that everybody had to use sooner or later. It was not subject to fashion or to economic upsets. And there was not very much that Pete missed when his services were called upon. Many a ring had been left on a finger and many a man had died in a shoot-out with plenty of money still in his pockets. Pete had spotted something about the death of Bill Conyers. He had said nothing to the others in the canyon, but once he and his son were alone, he told the lad of the discovery.

They were having a meal together at the back of his business premises while his wife ironed clothes upstairs.

'You and me is goin' back to that canyon, boy,' he

said quietly as he chewed at a tough piece of meat. 'There's gold to be had out there.'

The young man looked up from his plate. His fattish face was puckered in thought.

'But everybody in town says there's no gold there, Pa,' he said dubiously. 'I've been hearin' folks say it for months. Ever since old Bill Conyers set up camp at the canyon. They was all laughin' at 'im.'

The mortician gave a tight smile. 'And they was all wrong, lad,' he said cheerfully. 'Just because the old-timers think they worked out that canyon, don't mean they're in the right of it. Why in hell do you think some fella killed Bill Conyers?'

'To steal his poke. Don't you remember that his wife said it was missing?'

'Oh, sure. Sure,' his father said mockingly. 'And after he was dead, what did the killer do? He left a Colt worth thirty dollars and a shotgun worth almost as much. He was after gold, boy. And I figure as how there was enough of it to make him forget little things. A few extra dollars didn't matter no more.'

The lad shrugged. 'Could be, Pa,' he agreed reluctantly, 'but it might be that he was disturbed by someone or something.'

The mortician leaned across the table and pointed his knife at the youth.

'There was another thing, lad,' he said in a whisper. 'I saw the gold.'

19

He nodded vigorously and the knife shook with excitement. 'Where?' the youth asked eagerly.

'In the pan, boy. In the pan. When we was loadin' the wagon, I picked the thing up to empty out the dried gravel. There were flecks of gold dust in it. He must have been shot while he was kneelin' at the edge of the creek. The pan dropped out of his hand and then the water dried off as the sun shone on it. Look at this.'

Pete Weldon put down the knife and delved into his waistcoat pocket. He carefully drew out a tiny piece of gold, not much bigger than a shotgun pellet. He laid it on the flat of his hand and let the youth admire it.

'We're on to a good thing, lad,' he whispered. 'And we ain't goin' to let the rest of this town know about it until we've got our share of what's there.'

'Is it legal, Pa?'

'It will be. I'm no man to take risks in that direction.' The mortician snorted. 'I had a talk with Ma Conyers before she left town. We made ourselves one nice deal. I'm buyin' her three claims. They'll all be registered legal-like at the assay office in Tucson. She'll transfer them to you, me, and your ma.'

The young man thought about it for a moment and the effort showed in his face. The beans on his knife gradually slipped back on to the piece of steak as he worked out the problem.

20

'And we'll have it all, Pa?' he asked in awe.

'Sure as hell, son,' the older man grinned. 'I'm arranging for her to get two hundred and fifty dollars for each claim. She'll make the transfer and the Tucson bank will settle things. I don't want our thievin' mayor to get wind of anythin', and him bein' the only banker in town ain't exactly a help. I'm telegraphin' the money out of town through your Aunt Emmie's bank. That way our local Shylock don't know what the deal is all about. And you gotta keep a tight mouth on this. Only the family need know.'

'What about Aunt Emmie?'

'She thinks I'm buyin' land, and her bank in Rosario won't be interested in what we're doing.'

The young man's thinking was beginning to produce some results. The fork and knife were moving to and fro from his mouth almost automatically as he worked at it.

'Who's goin' to do the mining, Pa?' he asked with a certain uneasiness.

The mortician grinned wolfishly. 'Not us, boy,' he said. 'It's a job that needs skill, and that we don't have. The only diggin' you and me is concerned with is up at the burial ground. We'll get your Uncle Fred.'

Young Nathan nearly choked on his meat. 'Uncle Fred?' he gasped. 'But he's an old man, Pa, and some folk say he ain't all there in the head.'

'I ain't concerned with his head, boy. He's a miner, and he knows how to handle a pick and one of them pans, that's a damned sight more than we do. I'll give him a share of the deal, and he'll be only too pleased to do what he's best at. He's family, and better than that, he ain't a man for talking.'

'Well, if you say so, Pa.'

'I do say so.'

It was for that reason that Nathan was driving the rig with his father beside him on the sprung seat. They had all the tools and a supply of food hidden under a tarpaulin on the wagon, while Uncle Fred had ridden out earlier on his mule to approach the canyon discreetly from a different direction. Pete Weldon had planned it all very carefully. He intended to get as much gold out of the creek as possible before a rush started.

It was late afternoon when the three men finally met up in Riva Canyon. Old Fred had been waiting for a few hours, seated on the ground with a fire going and coffee boiling happily away. He was a small man in his sixties, with a dark, lined face, and bald head that shone in the sunlight. He wore a full white beard that was stained with tobacco and his clothes were as drab as the sides of the canyon.

'You sure took your time gettin' here,' he growled tetchily as he scrambled stiffly to his feet. 'A fella could starve while he waits for a meal around here.'

He helped them to unload the rig and then got

22

busy with a skillet and a pile of thick slices of bacon that he placed lovingly over the fire. The smell of the sizzling food filled the canyon and the old man kneeled in front of the skillet as though worshipping at some special shrine. Pete Weldon sat watching him as he and Nathan quenched their thirsts with the scalding coffee. They listened to the noise of the bacon and the steady trickle of the creek through the echoing walls.

When the meal was cooked and laid out on a tin plate across his bony knees, old Fred finally paid attention to his two companions for the first time.

'There ain't no gold around here,' he said as he ate greedily. 'It was mined out years ago, just like I've been tellin' you all along. But you educated fellas is too full of yourselves to listen to an old-timer who's got the experience that don't come outa books. You're wastin' your cash, Pete. There's nothin' here.'

'I found gold,' the mortician insisted as he pulled the little nugget out of his pocket. 'You can't deny what's in front of your eyes.'

'Could have been dropped. It ain't a proof that there's pay dirt in the creek.'

Nathan put down his empty coffee-mug. 'That Conyers fella was killed for it,' he said thoughtfully. 'That must mean something. And his poke was missing. Weren't it, Pa?'

Pete Weldon nodded eagerly. 'You've the right of

it there, son,' he agreed. 'And don't forget that there was some dust in the pan when I cleaned it in the creek. That couldn't have been dropped by accident.'

Old Fred scratched his jaw. 'Well, I ain't sayin' it's not possible,' he conceded reluctantly, 'and there could be traces left from the old days. Some may even have come down from the hills after a flash-flood. But the signs ain't right. I don't get that special feelin' about the place.'

He glanced round the canyon and resumed eating while father and son drank some more coffee. Pete Weldon got up and threw the dregs of his mug into the stream. He stood at the edge of the water, looking down and letting it lap his boots.

'This is the spot where we found Conyers,' he said as he pointed. 'The pan was here, just on the edge of the water, so he must have been workin' at this point.'

Old Fred rose complainingly to his feet, cleaned the tin plate carefully in the sand, and then joined them by the water. He stared down at it as though looking for inspiration before going to pick up the metal pan that had been unloaded from the rig. He knelt on the edge of the swiftly flowing stream and scooped some of the gravel into it. The pan swung rhythmically in his experienced hands while he swirled the liquid around. His breathing came heavily and the bleary eyes strained to see what

24

was happening in the pan.

Father and son watched avidly as the old prospector ran his finger through the final residue before casting it back into the stream with an expression of disgust. He did it three more times before suddenly giving a little grunt of satisfaction. When he looked up at the others, the old eyes were alight with the gleam of success.

'Well, I guess you were right, Pete,' he said. 'There is gold here and as fine a dust as a man could wish to see.'

They could see the tiny flecks lying in the pan among the heavy particles of gravel. They had hit pay dirt. Young Nathan let out a whoop of delight while his father took the news with only a slight smile on his gaunt face.

'Well, I ain't wasted my money,' the mortician said with grim satisfaction. 'We're the owners of three claims along this creek, and I'm goin' to take out two more, Fred, for you and your son. That way, we'll be able to dig out our fair share before anybody else comes hornin' in.'

'Ain't got a son,' the old man said glumly. 'You know full well that young Joe was kicked in the head by a mule.'

'Sorry, I forgot,' the mortician said cheerfully, 'but you know it, and I know it. Them fellas in the assay office don't. The more registered claims our family have got, the better. We gotta do all this legal and proper so that there'll be no claim-jumpin' when the word gets out.'

'And I does all the work?' Fred asked bluntly.

'Just until we know how we stand. Young Nathan can come out and help now and then, but he can't leave town too often. Folk would begin to wonder.'

The three men looked round the canyon with an air of ownership. None of them noticed the watcher who was levelling a Winchester carbine at them from behind a rock.

THREE

The watcher took careful aim and pulled the trigger. The noise echoed from the reddish walls of the canyon and scared up a swirling mass of small birds. A jackrabbit scuttled for cover while the bullet ploughed into the water and sent up a spray that hit old Fred in the face and shoulders.

All three men stood petrified for a moment, and then, as though sprung from traps, they ran for cover. The prospecting pan was tipped over; the dust was lost, and only a deep silence followed the explosion.

'Where the hell did that come from?' Pete Weldon whispered anxiously. 'I don't see nobody.'

Fred was kneeling behind a rock a few feet away. He had drawn an old Army Colt and the hammer was pulled back ready for use. His voice had the calm of an experienced old-timer.

'I ain't rightly sure,' he said, 'but he's holed up somewhere ahead and he's certainly got the drop

27

on us. We gotta get to the mules and hightail it outa here before he starts up again.'

Pete Weldon had a sudden rush of courage as he snorted angrily. 'And let the bastard scare us off?' he grunted. 'This is our gold and we got it legal-like.'

'Well, if you want to go out and tell him that, fella, I wish you luck,' the old man chuckled. 'But until we know where the hell he is and how many others he might have with him, I'm all for playin' it safe. Have you got a gun?'

Pete Weldon produced his small derringer and Fred looked at it with disgust.

'I think there's a shotgun on the rig,' young Nathan chipped in from where he lay half-buried in some bushes.

The old man grimaced. 'And the rig is sure one hell of a way down the canyon. We just gotta back off quietly as best we can, so keep your heads down and hope he don't aim no better with his next shot.' Almost as he said the words, another explosion rent the quietness. Large chips of rock flew off the boulder behind which Pete Weldon lay. He let out a startled yell and tried to get closer to the reddish earth. His little moment of courage was fast evaporating.

'You got the right of it there, Fred,' he muttered in an unsteady voice. 'I hate to leave all our gear behind, but I reckon as how we got no choice.'

There was a large clump of mesquite just behind

28

them and the three men warily crawled the few yards needed to get among the dusty foliage. They dared not risk looking out in case the marksman tried again. There was a long silence in which a solitary bird settled above their heads on a sandstone ledge and looked down at the scene as it preened its feathers.

The noise of the hoofbeats echoed the length of the canyon and gradually faded into the distance. Old Fred raised his head cautiously and looked around. There was a faint haze of dust where a curve in the crumbling walls hid the northern end of the gorge. He got slowly to his feet and holstered the old Colt.

'I reckon he's gone,' he said quietly.

The other two still sheltered behind the mesquite while he walked stiffly over to the fire and picked up the coffee-pot.

'Are you sure he's gone?' Pete Weldon called anxiously from his safe position.

'Well, he ain't shot me yet, has he?' the old man mocked. 'Come on out and let's swill a little of the dust from our throats. Then I figure as how we head away for town in case he comes back with a few friends. We can always return another day. With more firepower.'

After drinking their coffee, the three turned the rig around, cleared away all signs of their visit, and started back for Halo Township.

Pete Weldon was a bitter man. He felt that nothing would induce Fred to work the gold all by himself if there was any danger of a claim-jumper who carried a rifle and intended to use it. He would have to think out a new plan for exploiting the canyon and its treasure. It was late evening by the time they reached town. The place had a livelier air than usual. There seemed to be more people on the streets and more horses tied outside the two saloons and the Austin House hotel. Pete Weldon sensed the change in atmosphere as he and his son got down from their rig and began to unhitch the mules. Old Fred had already gone his own way to the little hut at the edge of town where he spent his days with a large dog and a stone jar of corn mash.

'You tend to things here, Nathan,' Pete said as he shook his hat to remove some of the dust. 'I'm gonna ask a few questions around town. There's somethin' happenin' here and it might mean a bit of business comin' our way.'

The youth grinned. 'We got old Ma Gridling's casket ready for use, Pa,' he said happily. 'She seems keen on seein' out the month. We can always make it do for someone else. So long as they ain't too tall.'

His father snorted. 'The old bitch will see out the year just to spite us. Now, don't forget to feed them mules. They've worked hard today.'

30

He went stalking off through the darkness of the side-lanes to the brighter noisiness of the main street. The Golden Globe saloon was busy and somebody was playing the rarely used piano. He could see several knots of people gossiping on the board walks, and, to his surprise, the hardware store was still open. He walked across to it and peered through the doorway.

Jake Fenton was behind the counter serving a couple of men with shovels and picks. He glanced round as Pete Weldon entered and gave him a cheerful greeting.

Being cheerful was Jake's line of work. He was short and stout, and as he himself put it, he was too fat to run and too fat to fight. For that reason he tried to be friendly to everybody, and it paid off. He was the most popular man in town and his sweating round face, full red lips and dyed hair, that matched the large moustache, were universally known.

Pete Weldon watched the two men leaving. They were not locals and he pursed his thin mouth in puzzlement at why they should be buying hardware so late in the evening.

'What's happenin' in town, Jake?' he asked as casually as he could.

The fat man grinned and spread his hands in an all-embracing gesture of goodwill.

'You've not heard the rumour then?' he asked.

'Some damned fool claims to have found gold out in Riva Canyon. I don't know how the story got around but fellas have been comin' in from miles away and I've sold more goods in the last hour than I've sold all day. Phineas Cutler's kept his general store open as well.'

Beads of sweat broke out on Pete Weldon's forehead.

'It's all nonsense,' he said tersely. 'Somebody's havin' us for a bunch of rubes. There ain't no gold in Riva Canyon. Ain't been for years.'

'Maybe so, Pete, but it sure as hell is good for business.'

The mortician said no more in case he gave himself away. He crossed the street to the marshal's office and paused for a moment on the porch to get back his customary poise. Dave Anders was sitting at his desk with a cup of coffee steaming at his elbow while he read a Tombstone newspaper by the light of two oil lamps. He looked up anxiously at being disturbed so late in the evening.

'Oh, it's you, Pete,' he said with a note of relief in his voice. 'I thought somethin' might be happenin' out on the street. It's sure noisy enough out there tonight.'

'Jake Fenton tells me that there's a rumour goin' round of gold bein' found in Riva Canyon. Who started that story, Dave?'

The lawman shrugged and took a sip of his

coffee. 'It seems to have started with some fella goin' into the Golden Globe for a drink,' he said without interest. 'Told them that he came across dust in the creek that runs through the canyon. Can't be true. The place was worked out years ago.'

Pete Weldon nodded eagerly. 'That's what I told Jake,' he said.

His voice held a note of anxiety that the lawman noticed instantly. 'Why the interest?' he asked.

The mortician hesitated for a moment, and then made a decision. He sat down in front of the desk.

'I gotta tell you, Dave,' he said quietly. 'When Ma Conyers left town, she was right low-spirited. I felt real sorry for the poor woman.' He paused for effect. 'So I did somethin' mighty stupid. I bought the three claims she owned. They're bein' sorted out at the assay office right now.'

Dave Anders took hold of his coffee cup and raised it to his lips. He was trying very hard not to smile.

'That was a generous thing to do, Pete,' he said. 'You stand to lose all the money you paid. I hope it wasn't too much.'

'No, not really. Just enough to help the poor woman on her way. But the point is, if gold is discovered there, then I'd be ownin' three claims. There's folks around town who are buyin' shovels and pans from Jake Fenton. They're stockin' up on food as well from Phineas Cutler. If there's a rush on that canyon, where do I stand?'

The marshal nodded his head. 'I see your problem, Pete. They wouldn't be likely to respect your claims, even if you put markers down. You could be left right out of it unless you were on the spot, diggin' and dredgin' along with the rest of them.'

The mortician stood up angrily. 'I've got legal rights, ain't I?'

'Sure you have, but how in hell do you enforce them? I got no real authority out there, and even if I had, do you think folks hungry for gold would take any notice of me? Hell, I'd be knocked down and trod under in the rush. The only thing you can do is to hightail it out there and work your claims. Take plenty of firepower, and a few folk you can trust. that's the best advice I can give.'

Pete Weldon went stalking angrily back to his home a few minutes later. His son was eating supper, and his wife, ever patient, put out a meal for her irritable husband without asking any questions.

She pointed wordlessly to a piece of paper that lay on the table. It was a message from the telegraph office to the effect that Ma Conyers had seen the official at the assay office and the new claims would be following by stage in the next week or so.

Pete Weldon cursed luridly. A message like that was the last thing he needed. No mention of claims or assay office should have been included. No wonder the town knew that there was gold in Riva Canyon.

He went to bed miserably without finishing his supper.

That was a mistake. He missed seeing the dozen or so men who left Halo Township at various times during the night. Some had light rigs drawn by mules and horses. Some had loaded their gear onto their mounts. But all were going in the same direction with the intention of finding gold. The rush had started.

FOUR

Marshal Anders watched them go. He was biting his lip with worry at the exodus and what it might mean to law and order. He still could not believe that there really was gold in Riva Canyon, but the rush out there, and the inevitable fights over claims, would cause him a few headaches.

He retired to his office, drank some coffee, and paced up and down restlessly. Any desire for sleep had gone, and he kept returning to the window each time another horse or wagon passed on its way to the canyon. He finally made up his mind to do something and began to load his guns.

Half an hour later he mounted his mare to ride out of town in the direction that had been taken by the prospectors. Dawn was already showing itself behind the long range of hills and the noises of the night were giving way to the calls of birds leaving their perches among the vegetation and going off to look for food. He rode at a brisk pace, hoping to get to the canyon before they started disputing the areas that each would work. He had some vague idea that his authority might just about keep the peace and allow his fellow townsmen to look for gold without killing each other in the process.

The canyon was reached by mid morning. He entered the wide entrance between the sloping walls to hear the hoofbeats of his horse echoing eerily as it moved. He drew rein and listened. There was no sign of life, and it puzzled him. Then he heard a slight noise from around the next bend. It was the neigh of a horse and his brow relaxed a little. They were there all right, but why was there no noise from them? He had expected to hear picks and shovels being used, or to hear squabbling or even gunfire. He rode on slowly, rounding the bend in the canyon to confront the wagons left nose to tail along the side of the fast-running creek. Horses and mules grazed nearby or drank from the clear water. There were no signs of any human beings.

The marshal got down from his horse. He was sweating now as he swung the clip from the top of his holster. He advanced slowly along the canyon, watched by the animals as he moved silently on the mixture of coarse grass and shingle that lined the edges of the creek. Then he came upon them as he rounded the next curve. They all sat or stood silently as if at a church meeting. All the men who had rushed madly from town ready to dig for gold

cowed men standing there in an agitated group. The marshal walked slowly along the edge of the creek until he reached the far end of the canyon where the walls fell away and gave out on to a rising plain of dense grass that was seared by the hot sun. Hills rose in the distance, shrouded in a blue haze as though suspended in space.

There was no sign of any marksman among the rocks or in any of the clumps of mesquite. He had not expected to find anyone and his movements were only a gesture to show that he was doing his duty.

When he returned to where the men were gathered, it was clear that the nervousness was dying and that greed was taking over again. They were unpacking their gear, picking out areas for exploring, and the arguments were starting as their voices grew louder and all sense of friendship was forgotten.

Two of them did spare the time to help Dave Anders to get the body across the back of the old man's mule. This work was ignored by the rest of the crowd. Their eyes were bright now with the prospect of gold, and the removal of a corpse was of little interest. There would be more corpses if they could not agree about sharing out the claims.

Dusk was falling and Halo Township was quiet when the marshal arrived leading a mule with a dead body across it. A few people stared and some children followed him to the office of the mortician. Young Nathan Weldon saw what was happening from the window and rushed to tell his father. The two men came hurrying out to the stoop, their faces alive with the prospect of doing business.

It was Pete Weldon who first spotted the identity of the man lying across the back of the mule. He let out a strangled cry and his gaunt face twitched at the sight.

'My God, Dave!' he gasped as he touched the body gingerly. 'How did this happen to Fred?'

Dave Anders told him where the old man was found and then helped the two morticians carry the corpse into the building and through to one of the tables in the rear room.

'When did you last see Fred?' he asked as they started undressing the body.

'See him?' The question seemed to have taken Pete Weldon by surprise. 'Well, yesterday, I reckon.'

'At Riva Canyon?'

There was an uncomfortable silence as father and son looked at each other. The mortician nodded glumly.

'We took him up there to do the digging,' he admitted, 'but some fella started shootin' at us and we had to back off.'

The marshal was interested now. 'And Fred was killed?' he asked.

'Hell, no. We kept our heads down till this

shootin' fella gallops off, and then we pack everythin' up and make for home in case he's got any friends close by. Fred was with us all the way. I came through town with Nathan but he went round the back way so as not to call attention to what we'd been doing in the canyon. I didn't want the whole town to know we'd been lookin' for gold. Even though I got legal rights there.'

Dave Anders picked up the discarded leather waistcoat and flannel shirt. He examined the hole and the bloodstains.

'Well, he weren't shot at close range,' he mused, 'and he ain't rigid no more, so I reckon as how Fred went back there by hisself to start a bit of diggin' or panning. Maybe he intended to cut you out.'

Pete Weldon's mouth tightened. 'The scurvy, ungrateful son of a bitch,' he growled. 'I should have known the old devil would try somethin' like that. Well, it ain't done him a whole lot of good.'

He looked sharply at the lawman.

'How come you was out there, Dave?' he asked suspiciously.

'I just followed the crowd,' the marshal told him. 'There are about twenty of the locals and a few strangers out in the canyon, and they all seem to be after the gold.'

The mortician let out a groan of despair. 'What about my rights?' he complained.

The marshal smiled. 'They won't count for much

against all their guns,' he told him cheerfully.

Young Nathan was finishing the job of undressing Fred's body and the lawman leaned forward to look at the wound.

'Dig the bullet out for me, Pete,' he said softly.

The mortician stared at him with surprise written all over his face.

'And why the hell should I be doin' that?' he asked. 'It's a doctor's job.'

'I want it done, so get on with it.'

'But it's a medical job, Dave. I ain't equipped for that sort of thing.'

'You're well enough equipped when it comes to removin' gold rings. Now, get me that bullet.'

Pete Weldon shrugged his shoulders and went over to a wall cupboard. He removed a leather bag that was very much like that carried by the medical profession. It contained a full set of surgical tools and it took him only a few minutes to probe the wound and proudly display a slightly damaged bullet between the jaws of an extractor.

'I reckon this to be a .44 or .45, don't you?' Dave Anders said as he held it up to the light.

'I guess so.'

'And all you ever owned was a derringer and a shotgun, Pete. I figure that lets you out.'

The mortician thought about it for a moment and then brightened up a little.

'Yeah, I see what you mean now,' he said. 'But I

wouldn't have killed Fred, no-how. Point is though, Dave, who the hell did kill him?'

The man who killed him was now miles away. He was a young fellow who rode a small bay cow pony. His saddle was of good quality and he was dressed in clean, store-bought clothes. He had a childish face; open and rather simple, with a broad nose and tow-coloured hair that grew low on his forehead. He rode well, his hands firm on the reins and his pale blue eyes watering in the wind.

As he breasted a rise, the ranch lay before him. He had already been on his father's land for the last half-hour and was now approaching the fine ranch house laid round a courtyard in the Mexican style. He came through the large gates and drew to a halt before the wide porch that fronted the whitened building and was bright with pot plants.

A Mexican ran out from an adjoining shed to take charge of the sweating animal while the young man knocked the dust from his shoulders and hat before going into the house.

It was a pleasant place that smelled sweet and he entered a room where his father sat in a deep leather chair reading the latest newspaper from Tucson. The man looked up at his son's arrival and put the paper down on a low table.

Joe Jenkins was a big man with a red face and

fierce white moustache. His grey hair was plentiful and still had darker streaks in it despite his sixty-odd years. He looked at his son with a certain impatience.

'Well, boy, what the hell is you doin' back here?' he demanded in a harsh, gravelly voice. 'I told you to stay out there and keep an eye on that place.'

Young Lew was afraid of his father and visibly cringed at the older man's loud voice.

'I done what you said, Pa,' he spluttered, 'but a fella came pannin' for gold, just like you said they might. So I shot him.'

'Shot him!' The rancher bounced out of the chair and grabbed the young fellow by his collar.

'I didn't tell you to go killin' folks!' he roared. 'All you had to do was watch the canyon and see if anythin' was happenin' there. Who in hell did you shoot?'

'I don't know. Some old fella. He had all the mining stuff and he was panning the creek just like they did years ago. Then the others arrived. You wanted 'em scared off, Pa, and I figured shootin' him would do it.'

The rancher released his son's collar and stepped back a little.

'What others?' he asked. 'What others arrived?'

'Well, after I shot the old fella, I climbed down to the creek to see if he had any gold in the pan. There weren't none so I reckoned as how I'd get a few hours' sleep and then have a meal. Nothin' else seemed to be happenin' and I decided to head for home. As I rides round the edge of the ridge on the south side of the canyon, there's a dust cloud in the distance. So I hangs on and waits to see who's on the trail.'

The rancher looked at his son with impatient ferocity. 'And who in hell was on the trail?' he snapped.

'A real crowd of fellas from the direction of Halo Township. There was horses and wagons and they sure was goin' hell for leather to reach the canyon. We got a gold rush there, Pa. Just as you said.'

Joe Jenkins seemed to lose something of his fierceness. He went back to the chair and sat down heavily.

'Did they see you?' he asked after a long silence.

The lad shook his head. 'No, siree. I kept down below the ridge and high-tailed it back here fast as fast. I reckon that dead body will put a scare in them though.'

'Only for a time, lad. Only for a time. If there's gold there, they'll soon get over any worries about the odd shooting. Folks can get mighty brave when there's gold to be had.' He looked up at his son. 'You did wrong, boy,' he said in a low voice. Then his fierce eyebrows knitted angrily. 'You didn't shoot that Conyers fella as well, did you?' he asked in sudden alarm.

45

'No, Pa, I never went near the place until you sent me there after all the local folks started talkin' about gold in Riva Canyon. You said that he was just a no-good fool who didn't know the place was worked out years ago.'

'Yeah, that's what I said, sure enough. And I was wrong. If they start findin' gold again, we've got trouble on our hands.'

The young man frowned heavily as if trying to work it all out.

'I don't see how, Pa,' he said. 'We got plenty of water. What does the Riva Canyon creek matter to us?'

The rancher looked at him in despair. 'Lookit, boy,' he snapped. 'Twenty years ago we were nearly ruined by the rush for gold in Riva Canyon. Our cattle need that creek flowin' clear and fast.

'Once those prospectin' fellas start diggin' and panning, the water turns to a thick, yeller mud you could build bricks with. The other streams can't make up for the loss. Your grandpa and me was hard put to survive. Cattle need water, and we can't afford a situation like that again. Our cattle started making for streams on the McCready spread. It nearly caused a range war.'

'What can we do then, Pa?'

Joe Jenkins heaved a sigh and looked suddenly old.

46

'We go have a word with Sam McCready, and then we close down that canyon.'

FIVE

Riva Canyon was full of noise. The sounds of digging and talking echoed along its length and there was a fine dust in the air that settled on the sweating men who worked along the creek or on the slopes of reddish stone.

There were horses and mules cropping the sparse grass, and near the southern mouth of the canyon, two wagons from Halo Township were trading any goods that the miners might need. Jake Fenton had arrived from his hardware store, his big moustache marking him out from the crowd as he went around telling the working men of his supplies of tools. Phineas Cutler was there too, his wagon loaded with food and drink which his son sold eagerly from the tailboard.

Phineas Cutler was a short, solid-looking man with a flat, dark face and small nose above a shrewd mouth that was usually clamped tightly on a small cigar. His eyes were alight at the amount of business he was doing, and he moved up and down the canyon to remind everybody of what he had to sell.

The creek was running like some muddy, open sewer. The water had been stirred by all the workings with picks and pans and by the tramping of animals. There were no marked claims and the prospectors worked where the fancy took them.

There had been small finds in the two weeks of gold hunting. Tiny nuggets had turned up now and then with small traces of dust in the water that kept hopes rising for a big discovery.

Phineas Cutler drew closer to Jake Fenton and took him by the elbow.

'I been doin' one good trade this coupla weeks,' he said in his hoarse, gravelly voice. 'Better than stayin' in town and waiting for folk to come to me. This little shindig could be the makings of us, Jake.'

The hardware store owner did not answer right away. He took a deep breath and looked round the canyon.

'You may be right,' he said quietly, 'but I remember the last gold finds. A lotta people died.'

The food supplier shrugged. 'So they go a little loco.' He laughed. 'That's what gold does to folks. You and me has to reap the harvest while it's there, fella.'

Jake Penton made no answer. He did not like his

49

colleague and considered him a dishonest rogue who gave short measure, despised the small town, and spent too much time drinking in the saloons. He suddenly realized that a silence had fallen over the scene. He looked round at the suddenly frozen attitudes of the prospectors. They stood poised like statues amid the eerie stillness while only the horses and mules continued to graze unheedingly.

All eyes were fixed on a point near the north end of the canyon. A group of horsemen filled the width to block any exit, and when Jake Fenton glanced in the opposite direction, he could see another mass of riders at the far end of the red-walled gorge.

'What the hell in tarnation is goin' on here?' Phineas Cutler shouted belligerently. He reached for the .44 at his belt, and as he did so, a shot rang out.

The noise echoed from rock to rock and a spurt of red dirt shot up near the food-dealer's feet. He hurriedly took his hand away from the butt of the gun.

Joe Jenkins of the Double J ranch sat his large horse like some monumental block of stone. A Winchester was cradled in his right elbow and half a dozen ranch hands were lined up behind him.

Fifty yards to the south was the other group of riders, equally menacing and headed by the rotund figure of Sam McCready. The boss of the S bar M was hunched in his saddle like some little black beetle. He carried a shotgun and his men were all armed with carbines.

'Now, we ain't out to kill nobody,' Joe Jenkins shouted in his stentorian voice, 'but we aim to put a stop to this diggin' for gold. So you folks just pack your goods and take yourselves off before things get ugly.'

There was a silence for a few moments and then a growling noise seemed to fill the canyon as the thirty or so prospectors found their voices and their courage. The horsemen levelled their carbines and some of them, young and not used to fighting, looked more nervous than the gold-hunters.

'And who the hell are you to come tellin' us what to do?' a voice came from the creek. There was a loud echo of support and the horses stirred uneasily.

'I'll tell you who I am,' Joe Jenkins shouted. 'I'm the fella what gets this creek flowin', like a tide of yeller mud all over my land. The cattle can't drink it and go wanderin' off to my neighbour's water. Well, that causes trouble, and last time it happened, we was shootin' each other instead of shootin' the gold-hunters. Well, this time, we aim to do it different. We'll shoot you folks instead. It's your choice.'

'You got no rights in this!' somebody shouted from a position where he was hidden behind the others.

51

'I got rights!' Joe Jenkins shouted back angrily. 'And they come outa this gun. Now get on your horses and head for home while you still can.'

There was a loud clicking of hammers being drawn back as the horsemen prepared to shoot. It was enough to start the prospectors scrambling around, emptying their gravel-filled pans, and gathering up the spades, blankets and saddles as they began to head for their horses. Jake Fenton turned smartly towards his wagon where his assistant was already raising the tailboard. Only Phineas Cutler stood his ground. His face was expressionless as he stood as though waiting for something to happen.

It soon did. As one of the older gold-hunters was washing out his pan in the creek, he suddenly let out a yell.

'Gold!' he shrieked joyously in his cracked voice. 'I've found a nugget! A big one!'

The other men gathered round him. There was a babble of excited voices as the menacing horsemen at each end of the canyon were forgotten. The old-timer was holding up a piece of gold. It was not some tiny pellet but a really substantial nugget. His fingers were trembling as he showed it around.

It was Phineas Cutler who pushed his way through the mob and took the trophy from the old man's hand to cast an expert eye over it. He weighed it amid a sudden silence, bouncing it up and down on his large palm and pursing his mouth judicially as he gauged the value. 'Over two ounces,' he said, 'and as nice a piece as you'll ever see. Where'd you find it?'

'It was right there in the creek as I cleaned out my pan,' the old man said in a tremulous voice. 'Just on the edge of those stones. I near trod it into the ground, I did. What's it worth?'

Phineas Cutler weighed it again in his hand. 'Well,' he said slowly, 'I'd say at a guess that there's at least forty dollars there. Quite a find, fella.'

Somebody whistled and the hubbub grew again as the men began picking up courage to face the ranchers and their mounted hands.

'I couldn't earn that in a month,' somebody said in a loud voice.

Everybody turned to stare at the speaker. It was one of the ranch hands who had lowered his shotgun and was in the act of getting down from his horse. Joe Jenkins swung on him angrily.

'Stay in your place, boy!' he roared. 'We ain't here to play games. We're here to clear this lot out before they ruin our water supply.'

The man hesitated, but as he clutched the pommel of his saddle, he saw that the other horsemen across the canyon were also restless. One of them was already down on his feet, running towards the creek. His boss, Sam McCready, swore luridly and put spurs to his horse to chase the man.

53

He caught up with him at the edge of the water and reached down with his shotgun to strike the errant ranch hand with the barrel of it. The blow took the man across the side of the face and he fell backward into the stream.

There was a strange rumbling of sound as other ranch hands moved their horses forward. Sam McCready found himself being pressed nearer to the creek, hustled by his own men as he watched the fellow he had struck getting to his feet. Blood poured down the man's face as he stood, drenched with water, in front of his boss.

'Now, get back to your horse and let's have some sense around here!' Sam McCready bawled. He turned to the others who were crowding him and making his horse restless. 'And the rest of you get back and give us some room.'

The man standing in the stream was moving his jaw tenderly. 'I ain't goin' no place,' he said slowly, 'and I ain't takin' a beatin' from nobody.'

He drew his Colt as he spoke, and before his boss could level the shotgun, a bullet took Sam McCready in the side of the neck and he tumbled from his horse. There was a silence as everybody watched the water stain with blood. The owner of the S bar M stirred for a few moments and then lay dead. His killer still stood in the middle of the creek, looking slightly scared at what he had done.

'I reckon he had it coming,' somebody said to

break the silence.

There was a mutter of agreement, and fifty yards away, Joe Jenkins looked at his own men and saw the looks on their faces. He knew when he was beaten.

'I'm headin' out,' he said in a flat voice to Lew. 'This can be settled another day.'

He turned his horse and led the way back through the canyon to the open pasture beyond. Most of his men followed but a few remained behind to try their luck with the gold. Two of Sam McCready's men gathered up his body, put it across the horse and led it back through the other end of the canyon. Some of his men also stayed behind, and all of a sudden, things went back to normal as if nothing had happened to spoil the feverish seeking after gold.

Phineas Cutler still stood with the nugget in his hand. He and the old prospector had taken hardly any notice of the shooting. He was paying the old man a number of dollar bills after having weighed the nugget properly on a small brass pocket-scale that his son had brought from the wagon.

Jake Fenton looked on nervously. The shooting had upset him and he wanted to get out of the canyon and safely back to Halo Township as soon as possible. Although he did not like Phineas Cutler, he would welcome his company back to town. It was a long journey and he was carrying quite a lot of money from the successful trading he had done.

To his relief, the other storekeeper appeared to have completed his business and had gestured his son to mount the wagon to head back home. Jake Fenton breathed a sigh of gratitude as they left the canyon and headed south.

Phineas Cutler was sitting back on the sprung wooden seat of his rig with a slight smile of satisfaction on his flat, dark face. His son was driving, making the mules move as fast as possible to get home before nightfall. He glanced occasionally at his father as if thinking of saying something.

Young Will was a sturdy copy of his sire. He was short and squat with large hands, a flattish face, and broad mouth. His hair was almost blond and gave him something of the appearance of an overgrown baby. He plucked up courage at last.

'That nugget, Pa,' he said tentatively.

'What about it?'

'It looked just like the one you got from Uncle Billy when he owed you for all them vittals. He used to wear it on his watch chain.'

Phineas Cutler grunted. 'It is the same one, boy, but keep your fool mouth shut about it.'

The lad's brow puckered as he tried to work things out. His father took pity on him.

'Lookit, lad,' he said as he shifted in his seat, 'we're doin' good business in that canyon. More than we could ever do back in the store. In the past two weeks, all they've found is a few grains of dust. Enough to keep 'em interested but not enough to make this shindig last much longer. They gotta have somethin' to get het-up about. So I used that nugget.'

'But it cost you money, Pa.'

'That's business, son. I was carryin' it around with me all ready to drop in the creek if no more gold traces showed up. Then these ranch fellas arrived, so I didn't have no choice. If them prospectors had been scared off back there, we'd have lost some real good trade. So I dropped it just on the edge of the water where old Jamie Pullen was packin' his gear. He couldn't miss it, and even if he had, some other fella would have spotted it. We've kept things goin' for at least another few weeks. Time to make a killing, boy.'

'Old Sam McCready was killed, Pa,' Will said thoughtfully. 'He was killed because you planted that nugget.'

'A lot of folk are goin' to be killed before this is through, son,' Phineas Cutler said contentedly. 'Just let's make sure it ain't you and me.'

SIX

Mayor Penning sat behind his desk and looked at the men who had gathered around on the hard bentwood chairs. His large office was at the back of the bank and smelt strongly of tobacco and whiskey. The members of the town council shifted uneasily as they listened to his report on the happenings in Riva Canyon.

The mayor was a large man, his great stomach pushing against the edge of his desk and his pale waistcoat dusted with cigar ash.

He was almost totally bald but managed to have generous sideburns and a grey moustache above his blubbery lips.

· 'Well, that's the situation,' he said fretfully. 'Four weeks of grubbing for gold and three men are dead. There's little enough to show for it but they're all hoping to make a big strike either in the creek or in the tunnels they're digging out there. There are more than twenty men from this township wasting their time when they should be back at their jobs and making proper provision for their families like decent, law-abiding citizens.'

'What's the marshal doin' about it?' the grain merchant asked dryly.

They all turned to look at Dave Anders who was leaning against the door with his fingers hooked into his gunbelt.

'There's nothin' I can do,' he said quietly. 'There are near forty men out there now, and they're all ready to fight anyone who's fool enough to interfere. They've already scared off the ranch owners, and I've got no deputies. You won't pay for them.'

There was an embarrassed silence until the town lawyer nodded his wizened head.

'He's right there,' he snapped in his shrill voice. 'The folk won't supply the money for law enforcement, and we can't expect Dave to go making trouble out there all by himself. Besides, he hasn't got a legal position in this thing. He's town marshal and this is county business.'

'The county won't make a move,' the mayor argued. 'They tell me that they haven't got the men, and that they've got other problems that are more urgent. Sheriff Ellison said only the other day that we're lucky not to have had more trouble.'

'But what about Sam McCready?' somebody asked. 'He was killed out there.'

The mayor snorted. 'Sam McCready hit that fella

with a gun-barrel. It was a damn-fool thing to do. What the hell could you expect after that? Even if we did arrest the killer, no jury round here would convict him. What do you think, Eddie?'

The lawyer nodded agreement. 'Those ranchers are too high-handed,' he said grimly. 'Sam asked for it, and he sure enough got it.'

'How much gold has actually been found in the canyon?' Dave Anders asked.

Jake Fenton swivelled round in his chair to face the marshal.

'I was tryin' to figure that out,' he said, 'and I reckon as how about two hundred dollars' worth has been taken out. A few tiny nuggets, one big one that was found while I was there, and the rest in dust from the creek.'

'It isn't much for a month's work,' the lawyer said. 'It could all peter out if we just let things be. Maybe we should just wait until they get tired of making fools of themselves.'

There was a general nodding of heads. Jake Fenton and the grain merchant were making good money out of the activities, and the saloon-keeper did well when the men occasionally came into town. Interference from the marshal or the mayor was the last thing they needed.

'We gotta keep our eye on it, all the same,' the mayor insisted, reluctant to appear defeated.

'I'm drivin' out there tomorrow,' Jake Fenton

said soothingly. 'Phineas Cutler and his lad are goin' as well. We can report back.'

'Good idea,' the mayor said thankfully.

'I'll ride out with you,' Dave Anders suggested. 'There's nothin' much happenin' in town durin' the week.'

They all agreed on that plan and the meeting broke up when the whiskey bottles were empty.

The morning was slightly colder with a trace of snow on the distant hills. The air was still and the sky clear and hard. Jake Fenton drove his rig gently over the rough ground as the mules picked their way carefully with a jingling of harness. Phineas Cutler and his son were behind them, their larger wagon clattering along and raising more dust as its wheels ground the earth noisily.

Marshal Anders rode alongside Jake's wagon. He was amused to be accompanied by another rider who seemed out of place on a horse. The mortician rode a small cow pony and his tall, gaunt frame appeared like a disjointed marionette as he bounced around in the saddle. He would have liked to have used his rig and let his son drive, but there was business to attend to in Halo Township and somebody had to mind the store.

Pete Weldon was still mightily annoyed at losing his claims. He was hoping that by going along with the marshal, he might be able to assert some rights in Riva Canyon. There was not much hope of it, but he hated to see his gold being dug out or panned by a bunch of intruders.

He was really better at dealing with the dead than the living, and another thought at the back of his mind was that there might be one or more bodies that needed burying up at the canyon. Gold prospectors were pretty trigger-happy folks, and that made good work for a mortician. The thought almost cheered him up.

Travelling slowly with the mule-drawn wagons, they made the canyon just after noon. It had warmed up and there was a slight breeze with a haze of dust in the air as the little party entered the towering cleft that echoed to their wheels and harness. A few jackrabbits scattered at their approach while the smell of the stream roused the mules from their stolid indifference.

Dave Anders looked around with a puzzled expression on his face. Everything seemed too quiet as he rode ahead to turn in to the main body of the canyon where the prospecting was taking place. When he rounded the bend, there was a flutter of wings as a score of buzzards rose clumsily into the air and went off to settle on the craggy rocks above.

The canyon was deserted. The marshal sat his horse, looking about him in astonishment. The tools were there, the burned-out cooking fires, and several canvas tents and piles of saddlery. There were shirts and pants hanging from sticks to dry out after being laundered while a large enamel coffee-pot sat on a pile of long-dead embers as though waiting to be lifted by some eager hand.

The buzzards had been scavenging among the remains of food and they sat now looking down on the canyon with their bright eyes watching every movement the marshal made. He got down from his horse, aware that the two wagons were behind him, their occupants as silent and anxious as he was. Pete Weldon descended from his own little pony and stood beside the lawman as they stared round the empty canyon.

'Where in hell have they all gone, Marshal?' the mortician asked tersely.

'Damned if I know. Their rigs are here, but no mules or horses.'

The two other men came over to join them. Jake Fenton was chewing uneasily on his moustache while Phineas Cutler looked round with almost no expression on his flat, dark face.

Dave Anders bent down to touch the ashes of one of the dead fires. He lifted the lid of the coffee-pot and looked at some mule droppings.

'They've been gone two or three days,' he mused. 'When were you last here, Jake?'

'We come once a week,' the store-owner said uneasily. 'I don't like this, Marshal. It's mighty scary.'

'They've taken their horses but not the saddles,' Phineas Cutler said as he pointed at the equipment that lay around. 'That don't make much sense.'

The marshal nodded.

'Then they can't have got far,' he said quietly, 'and they've left all their tools.'

He indicated the picks and shovels that littered the canyon. Pans were still full of gravel, one of them lying in the creek half submerged in the running water.

The marshal moved forward. His footsteps were loud in the confining space of the walls of reddish stone. He rounded the next bend, followed at some distance by the others. His hand was ready to use the gun at his side, and he felt a tension at the eeriness of a place that should have been a bedlam of noise.

As he looked from left to right at the sandy, sloping mass of rock on either side of him, something moved up ahead. He stopped in his tracks, his right hand reaching instinctively for the butt of the Colt. It was a tall clump of mesquite that had shivered to cast a fine cloud of dust into the air. There was something behind it.

'Come out from there!' Dave Anders shouted hoarsely. His gun was levelled at the mass of bushes and the hammer was drawn back.

The clump moved again and the marshal caught a sudden glimpse of what was hidden there. He

64

gave an embarrassed grin and lowered the pistol. Phineas Butler and the other two men drew nearer as he parted some of the thick lower stems to disclose the flank of a horse that was tethered there. When the four men walked round to the other side of the shuddering clump, they got a good view of the animal and its companion mule. The two were fully harnessed and had been grazing contentedly on the lush herbage.

'They ain't been here long,' Phineas said as he looked at their droppings. 'You know what that means, Marshal?'

'Yeah, I do.'

Dave Anders raised the gun again while the other men drew their own weapons. There was an extra tension in the air now as they looked carefully at the fissures and hollows, and the shallow tunnels in the sides of the canyon. They eyed the other clumps of bushes with suspicion.

The mule bore a pannier on each flank and Dave Anders opened the woven straw covers to glance at the bulging contents. One container was half full of gunbelts and Colt or Remington pistols, the other held a few coffee-pots, some metal plates, and an assortment of tin mugs.

Phineas Cutler peered in and grabbed hold of one of the pistols.

'That belongs to old Tom Wallace,' he growled. 'His initials are on the butt.'

The mortician dug out an old Army Colt and waved it under the lawman's nose.

'This belongs to Fred Burney,' he said in an unsteady voice. 'He's had it since he did his fightin' in the war. What in hell's happened to them all?'

They stood in a silent group, almost fearing to move in the enclosed space of the canyon. The two animals grazed happily as though everything was normal and no atmosphere of tension filled the air.

'There ain't no carbines,' Phineas Cutler suddenly exclaimed as his eyes wandered restlessly over the scene. 'Where have they gone?'

As if in answer, there was a sudden noise some twenty yards ahead of them, close to the north end of the canyon. A trickle of gravel and sand spattered down the sloping wall from the dark entrance of old mine-shaft. The four men all pointed their guns in that direction and Dave Antlers moved carefully towards the spot.

The others followed well behind him, the tall mortician bringing up the rear with a small derringer trembling in his bony grasp.

'Come outa there!' the marshal yelled as they stood below the steep slope which was covered by a mixture of scree and tight clumps of grass.

'It might just be an animal,' the mortician ventured uneasily.

'Then he owns a horse and a mule,' Phineas Cutler reminded him, 'and he hid out when we arrived on the scene.'

The mortician bit his lip in anger at his own stupidity. He kept behind the bulk of Jake Fenton and was relieved when the marshal sent him back down the canyon for the lawman's Winchester. Pete Weldon hurried away to fetch the carbine and returned to pass it to Marshal Anders who holstered his pistol and cocked the longer-range weapon,

He fired a single shot into the shadowy entrance of the small tunnel. A spurt of dust flew from the rocks followed by a moment of silence.

Then a short piece of something that looked like a tallow candle came tumbling down the slope. It bore a small fuse that spluttered angrily.

Dave Anders shouted a warning but the others did not need it. They all dived for cover as the stick of explosive tumbled towards the stream and blew up with a sharp roar that filled the canyon. A shower of small rocks and red dust rose like a curtain to clatter down on the four men who lay flat on the ground with their heads covered as best they could.

The horse and mule reared in panic behind the mesquite and tried to flee the scene. The cow pony managed it but the other animal was too well tied and had to stand trembling as the dust blew around it.

'We gotta get the hell outa here,' Jake Fenton muttered as he edged back down the canyon. The mortician was already crawling away and only Phineas Cutler seemed prepared to follow any lead the lawman set.

'He can't stay there for ever,' Dave Anders said grimly. 'We can wait him out. Only one of us needs to watch that tunnel at any one time. The others can be further back down the gorge. We can eat and rest while the heat gets to him. Are you with me, Phineas?'

'I am. I want them miners back here, and I figure as how this fella has scared them off in some way. That explosive stuff would do the job. It sure scares the hell outs me.'

'Me too. You go back to the rigs and tell our two heroes to set up camp and start makin' with some food. Take over from me in an hour.'

The store keeper nodded and backed slowly away while the marshal lay with the Winchester covering the tunnel mouth. It was quiet again now, The dust had settled and birds were hovering overhead. Dave Anders waited patiently for something to happen.

'You down there!'

The sudden shout after half an hour of silence took Dave Anders by surprise. He had almost dozed in the heat of the day and the call shook him guiltily awake. He levelled the carbine and waited.

'You down there!' the voice called again. 'I got a deal worked out.'

'So what's the deal?' the marshal shouted back.

'Bring my horse as near as you can to this tunnel. Make sure the girth's tightened, and then you and your friends go back to the other end. I'll come down with another few sticks of blastin' powder ready to use, you get well back round that next bend. If I can see anybody, I'll be throwin' things. You got that?'

'I got it, but it's no deal.'

'Why not?'

'There are four of us and more to come. We've got food and water, plenty of guns, and you're holed up neat as neat. You're stuck there, fella, and not all the blastin' powder in the county is goin' to get you outa there. So you just come down nice and quiet and I'll take you into Halo Township where I got me a jailhouse just waitin' for you.'

The man in the tunnel did not answer and the only sound was the running of the creek and the scraping of a lizard as it crawled past Dave Anders in pursuit of insects. He took out his gunmetal watch and looked at the time. He was feeling hungry and thirsty, anxious to get a spell by the wagons while someone else took guard. Phineas Cutler relieved him after a while and the marshal went back to where Jake Fenton had a fire going and a large pot of coffee bubbling happily away. The store-owner had fried some bacon to go with the thick pieces of fresh bread. He handed the plate over to the hungry man, who received it gratefully. Pete Weldon had already eaten and was dozing in the sun.

'That sure tastes good,' Dave said as he wiped his mouth. 'You cook well, Jake.'

The fat man grinned at the compliment. 'How's it goin' back there?' he asked.

'He's holdin' out but it can't last for ever. He's no place to go.'

The fat man leaned forward anxiously. 'Tell me, Dave,' he asked, 'what happened to all the folk back there? It's kinda weird.'

The marshal shrugged. It was a question that he had been asking himself.

'I reckon he scared them away with that blastin' powder, It's the only thing I can think of.'

'Their horses are missin' but not the saddles; ain't that a strange thing?'

'Maybe the blastin' powder scared them as well, so the folks had to move out on foot.'

'Then, why ain't they back in town, raisin' hell for the marshal? They had to go some place.'

Dave Anders grinned uneasily. 'Now, there you have me, Jake,' he admitted. 'I just can't figure it out at all.'

The stout man stroked his moustache. 'I don't like any of it,' he said. 'And this dynamite business. It could have been my own stock that fella was throwin' at us.'

70

The lawman jerked upright and nearly spilled his coffee. 'You supplied it?' he asked with sudden interest.

'Sure. I'm the only fella what stocks it in town. Why?'

'Jake, you wouldn't by any chance have some on your wagon right now?'

'Sure would. These prospectin' fellas always want a few sticks of dynamite. Why?'

'Because now I know how to shift that fella outa that tunnel real fast.'

The sun was getting low and the shadows were lengthening across the canyon. Dave Anders lay flat on his stomach above the sloping ridges of stone and looked down on the stream below and the curving sweep of the gorge with its clumps of mesquite and piles of excavated gravel and sand. He could see Phineas Cutler lying behind a rock with a rifle trained on the tunnel entrance that now lay some twenty feet below Dave Anders.

It had taken the marshal a sweating half-hour to scale the steep slope and then walk carefully across the grassy top of the canyon. He was now directly above the mouth of the little tunnel where their enemy lay concealed. He had gauged his position from the appearance of the opposite rocks and by watching for a signal when he was in the right

71

place. Phineas waved as the lawman appeared exactly above the tunnel. Dave waved back and then began to unfurl the long piece of rope that had two sticks of dynamite securely fastened to one end of it. The fuse had already been fitted by Jake Fenton. It was just the right length to give the lawman time to lower the explosive to the entrance before detonating.

The marshal lit the vesta with a slightly trembling hand. He had to protect it from the wind and he heaved a sigh of relief when the fuse started to spit like an angry bobcat.

He began to pay out the line rather quickly. He did not have Jake's faith in the time the fuse would burn and was anxious to get the dynamite away from himself as soon as possible. The sizzling bundle crept down the face of the canyon, bouncing from crag to crag until Phineas Cutler, watching every move, signalled that the tunnel entrance had been reached.

The arrangement was that it should be placed just above and out of sight of the man who hid there, and Dave Antlers hoped that they had got things right.

The explosion took him by surprise. It made the ground beneath him tremble as a great burst of dark material shot across the canyon and covered everything in dust. A few small pieces of rock flew above the marshal's head and one hit him on the back of the leg. He lay huddled for a moment before looking over the edge.

He could see nothing for the haze, but there was a rattling of scree and he could hear voices down below. He thought he heard a shot as he hurried back the way he had come. It was easier now but he sweated with the heat as he scrambled down the steep sides into the southern end of the canyon. He ran along the bank of the creek and past the wagons to where his three companions now stood, covered in a fine dust as they surveyed his workmanship.

A body lay in front of them, no longer moving and with a vivid burn across one side of the face. It was difficult to make out any details. The clothes were scorched and both hands damaged by the blast.

'What happened?' the marshal asked as he drew to a panting halt.

Phineas pointed up towards the tunnel mouth.

'He came tumblin' outa there,' he explained tersely, 'all burned by the blast. It blew down some of the entrance and he was too close for his own good. He came straight at us with his gun drawn, so I had to shoot him. Maybe it was the best thing. He looks to be hurt bad.'

Dave Anders looked at the .44 Colt that lay a few yards away. He bent over the body and felt in the pockets of the old waistcoat.

A few small coins and a little roll of banknotes tumbled out. Another pocket contained a small pouch of tobacco and a silver vesta box. It was the third pocket that surprised them all.

It also housed a small pouch, but it was not tobacco that fell into the marshal's palm. It was a trickle of shining gold-dust.

SEVEN

The mayor looked at the bag that lay before him. He sat behind his large desk with the marshal and Jake Fenton standing in front of him. Dave Anders had told the story of their adventure and the leading citizen had listened in complete bewilderment.

'Fifteen ounces,' he muttered as he poked the little bag with his finger. 'That must reckon out at about two hundred and forty dollars.'

'Near enough,' Jake Fenton agreed. 'Phineas Cutler weighed it and there ain't a doubt, John. That dead thief had done more than steal their rifles and horses. He got all their gold-dust as well.'

The mayor nodded. 'But where the hell are these people?' he asked. 'Some of them fellas is local and would have come back to town. They've got families here, and they can't have gone far without mules and horses.'

The mayor looked at the marshal for support.

75

'Could he have killed them all?' he asked. 'Is that possible?'

'There were no bodies and no blood,' Dave Anders said. 'I reckon he scared them off with the blastin' powder while their horses were spooked by the noise and bolted. The only odd thing is that it must have happened a few days ago and you'd have thought they'd have got back to town by now.'

'Why a few days ago?' the mayor asked.

'Well, we searched the canyon and there ain't no rifles there. This fella had already taken them away and had brought the mule back to load up with the rest of the guns and whatever else he could carry. He obviously took the most valuable stuff on his first trip.'

The mayor tapped nervous fingers on the desk-top.

'Do you reckon this fella was the cause of trouble from the start?' he asked. 'Do you think he killed Bill Conyers and then shot old Fred Weldon?'

The marshal shrugged. 'Could be,' he said doubtfully, 'but I don't see the point of it. It was shootin' them two that really started the rush. I figure as how we need to know what happened to them carbines.'

Jake Fenton and the mayor glanced at each other.

'Why?' they asked almost simultaneously.

'You gotta remember that he also had thirty-five

dollars in cash money on him. That's a mighty lot for a fella to be carryin' around on the range.'

'It could be part of the payment for sellin' the guns,' Jake Penton suggested.

'Exactly, and so could the gold.'

The mayor saw the point of the argument. 'So we need to know whether he robbed the miners of their dust or got it in payment for the rifles?' he suggested.

'That's my feeling,' Dave Anders agreed.

'Do we know who he is yet?' Jake asked after a moment for thought.

'No, I can't say as he's on any Wanted lists, but his face is a mess so there's no way of bein' certain. The only thing I got to go on is the panniers on the side of that mule. They're made of plaited reed, and the only folks doin' that sort of work round here are them Pueblo Indians along the San Isidro Valley. That mule could be from there as well. It's got no brand.'

'They wouldn't be buyin' guns,' the mayor said uneasily. 'They're all peaceful folk.'

'They're on the border,' Jake Fenton pointed out. 'The Mexicans buy guns.'

'You mean that they could be tradin' over the line?'

The marshal nodded. 'If they bought the guns off that fella, they could sell them on. Them Indians cross the border just like it ain't there. Nobody bothers them.'

'It would make sense too,' Jake Fenton interposed. 'Carbines are more important than pistols to the Mexicans.'

The mayor scratched his head as he thought about it.

'Well, I reckon there's not a lot we can do,' he said, 'but I sure as hell would like to know where all them fellas have gone.'

'I could ride out to the pueblo and have a word with the Indian agent,' Dave Anders suggested. 'He might know somethin' that would help us.'

Jake Fenton coughed. 'I've just thought of something,' he said, almost apologetically. 'It couldn't have happened the way we figured it.'

'What do you mean?' asked the mayor.

'Well, if that fella had chased them all outa Riva Canyon with dynamite, he had to have the dynamite when he arrived there. But that couldn't be the case. We found the rest of it in that mine tunnel and it was the stuff I supplied to the prospectors. So how did he get it from them?'

'Well – he could have held them up,' the mayor suggested.

'No, I see what Jake's gettin' at,' Dave Anders murmured. 'There were too many fellas there to be held up by one man, so what Jake is sayin' is that they'd all left the canyon before that fella even got there.'

'That's it.' The storekeeper nodded eagerly. 'And that makes it one hell of a puzzle.'

The marshal was getting ready to leave for the pueblo. The dead man had been buried, all the goods from Riva Canyon had been brought into town and stored in one of the cells at the back of the jailhouse, and Pete Weldon was almost smiling as he went about his business.

The mortician now had an empty canyon to exploit and had sent out his son and a couple of hired hands to start looking for gold on the claims that were legally his to search. Phineas Cutler and Jake Fenton had less to smile about. Without a gold rush, their businesses had slumped, and Phineas felt particularly annoyed after having spent so much in salting the area.

He fretted now in his store, determined to ride out there soon and place a few more tiny grains of gold where Pete Weldon's son would be likely to work. He needed to keep them hoping, and perhaps start another rush when local folk gathered up the courage to go out there again.

The marshal rode out of town a few days later. He had a long journey to the pueblo, going south through sparse pasture until he hit the broad river where the fertile land produced the crops the few remaining Pueblo Indians grew for their support. Their houses were of adobe, built in to the cliffs and steep slopes that had originally given protec-

79

tion from their enemies. The buildings were old now, and crumbling as the smaller population struggled to make a living in a world they no longer understood.

Dave Anders reached them on the second day. He pulled up his horse at the top of a long, sandy slope that led down to the row of cliffs where the sunbleached houses clung to the yellowish rocks. A woman was climbing up a short ladder to one of the dwellings and some children were playing with a puppy near a well. None of them took any notice of the stranger although a couple of dogs barked their defiance from a safe distance.

It was a white man who came striding out from a small wooden hut and advanced purposefully towards the marshal. He was a large fellow with a dark jacket and pants, his face reddened by the harsh sun and his grey hair was uncut, peeping out from under the broad beige Stetson. An old Colt hung high at his waist and he looked like he could use it.

'And what can we do for you, stranger?' he asked in a neutral voice.

Dave told him who he was. The man's attitude softened as he invited the marshal to step down from his horse and hitch it and the laden mule to a rail outside the small hut. They entered the tiny place through a curtained doorway and the lawman found himself in a clean and comfortable room where a stove stood in one corner with a coffee-pot bubbling on top of it. The man poured out a couple of scalding drinks and both men sat on either side of a plain deal table to sip the strong brew.

'I know the fella you're talkin' of,' the Indian agent said grimly. 'He came through here a few days back and his horse was festooned with rifles. Never did see so many guns on one animal. It was just right cruel. He exchanged one of them for that mule there and loaded the rest of 'em onto it. Wanted to sell all the guns here but I'm one strict Indian agent. I ain't havin' deals like that on my patch. Were they all stolen?'

Dave nodded and began to explain the details.

'Well, if that ain't the weirdest tale I ever did hear tell of,' the agent said as he shook his head in amazement. 'He never did bring ponies along with him. Them guns was the only thing he had. I reckon you got yourself one real problem there, Marshal. All them missin' men and their animals. Got any ideas?'

'No, but I figured as how, if he'd sold the rifles down here, the fellas he sold them to might know somethin' of his doings.'

The Indian agent grinned his agreement. 'He went across the border and sold them to Ed Whelan,' he said. 'And they don't come any worse than Ed Whelan. Heard of him, Marshal?'

81

Dave Anders nodded. 'Strikes me the name's been on quite a few posters,' he mused. 'He used to hold up stages, and had to go and live in Rosario a few years ago.'

'That's the fella. he's still there, and Rosario is only across the river from here. Hardly more than a spit and a holler away. What are you goin' to do?'

'I'm gonna visit Rosario.'

It was early evening when Dave Anders reached the outskirts of Rosario. It was a one-street town with three adobe cantinas, a couple of stores, a church that dominated a slight hill. and nothing much else. A smell of stale cooking-oil filled the air and a gentle wind blew dust down the centre of the main street in little swirls that gathered up dead leaves to spray them to the height of a man.

The marshal tied his horse to the rail of the largest cantina. He looked up and down the almost empty street before taking off his badge and stuffing it into his waistcoat pocket. The cantina was dark inside, the windows filthy and the floor covered in dirty straw. There were only a few men there and all of them were Mexicans. They looked at the foreigner with impassive faces and then turned back to their drinks as he walked out again.

He crossed the street to another cantina that huddled next to a two-storey boarding-house around which ran a rickety balcony.

Dave Anders could vaguely remember what Ed Whelan looked like. According to the Wanted lists, the fugitive from the law was a large man with a thick black beard and scars across his forehead. He would be instantly recognizable among the small, dark Mexicans.

The second cantina was almost as empty and smelt strongly of stale food. Faces were just as blank as the stranger was viewed, but in the far corner, there was one face that made Dave Anders catch his breath.

Ed Whelan was in town.

EIGHT

The man sat like an enormous toad at a small table. He made everything look small. The glass of tequila that sat in his large hand was like a thimble in his grasp, He had a dark beard that covered the lower half of the broad face and there were two livid scars across the furrowed, dark, forehead.

He was dressed like a preacher in long black coat and waistcoat, with a white shirt and black stock. A large gold chain crossed his paunch from pocket to pocket and his black hair was greased back to curl slightly above his collar.

Dave Anders took a deep breath before crossing the room and sitting down in front of the man.

'Ed Whelan,' he said. It was not a question. Just a simple statement.

Two dark eyes glared at him and one hand vanished under the table as if for a gun.

'Who wants to know?' The voice was low and wheezy, as if coming from a great depth.

'Somebody who might want to do business with you,' Dave Anders said quietly.

'What sort of business?' The eyes were wary and the large belly was heaving enough to move the table slightly.

'I've got some guns. Colt and Remington pistols. Complete with belts.'

'And why should I be interested in guns, fella?' The man's dark eyes were alert and hostile.

'I hear you bought some from a man who came into Rosario a short time back. He was sellin' rifles. Brought them in on an Indian mule.'

'I don't know from nothing, stranger. I just live quiet in this town. Who the hell are you, anyway? I ain't never seen you around here.'

Dave Anders leaned forward across the table, keeping his hands in view as he spoke in a low voice.

'I met a fella in Halo Township,' he said urgently. 'He had money to spend and was takin' a mite too much to drink for his own good. He told me that he'd been to Riva Canyon and got himself some rifles that he sold down here. I tried to stop him talkin' but the locals were lookin' mighty suspicious at strangers like us. He was a bit edgy and pushin' for a fight. He got into one later that night and some local fella shot him. I got the hell out while I could still make it. And then I went to Riva Canyon to see what he was talkin' about. His mule was there, and all these guns.'

85

The fat man's eyes flickered with interest for the first time. He swallowed his tequila at one gulp and motioned across the room for a refill.

'And what did you find at the canyon?' he wheezed.

'A lot of folks had been there, lookin' for gold. There were saddles, cookin' bits and pieces, and all these pistols. I took the guns and brought them down here. I ain't askin' big money, just a fair shake.'

'I ain't payin' big money, fella. Rifles is better than pistols this side of the border. They've got a revolution goin' on here and there's tradin' to be done if the price is right. Where are these guns?'

'On a mule a few miles back.'

The big man's mouth moved in what might have been a smile.

'Five dollars a gun,' he said.

Dave Anders snorted angrily and got up from the stool.

'You ain't the only market, fella,' he said as he made to leave.

'I'm the only one you've got. Now, calm down and let's talk some sense. Those guns are as hot as a kettle in Hades, but I can do you a trade, just like I did for Len Forman. These Mexicans don't have big money and they ain't easy to deal with. So you'd better make up your mind. I'm leavin' for the south early on Wednesday to do a little deal in Esqueda.

I don't aim to hang around here while you play hard to get. What's it to be?'

Dave Anders sat down again.

'I'll level with you,' he said slowly. 'The money ain't the only thing. I need somethin' else. If you can help me out, I'll agree to the price.'

His voice was humble and almost pleading as he sat listening to the fat man's heavy breathing at the other side of the table.

'And what would you be wanting?' Whelan asked.

'I was in Halo Township 'cos my pa had gone prospectin' in Riva Canyon. I'd been there before goin' into town, and found the place deserted. Not a man, not an animal. When I met up with Len Forman in the saloon and he started talking, I thought I'd be on to somethin' helpful. He got himself shot before he could tell me what happened back there, so I was no better off.'

'And you want to know what happened to your pa?'

'Yes.'

'And if I tell you what I know, we have a deal at five dollars a gun, includin' all ammunition and the belts?'

'Yes.'

Ed Whelan agreed to tell what he knew about disappearances in Riva Canyon.

Dave Anders spent the night in the Indian pueblo. He slept behind the little hut where the Indian agent lived. There was an awning of worn canvas that served as a veranda and the only things that disturbed his rest were the noises of the evening and a few vinegaroons that crawled over his feet from time to time.

The agent had doubts about the marshal's way of working, but the young lawman felt that the situation was desperate enough to make the risks worth while.

He set out for the border again early the next morning. The laden mule followed patiently behind bearing the panniers of loaded pistols. The arrangement was to meet at the outskirts of Rosario where money and information would be exchanged. Neither side trusted the other and Dave's mouth was dry as he neared the little town in the valley on the bend of the river.

He sat his mare and waited for several minutes before a small wagonette pulled by a single horse came out of the main street and moved towards him over the open grassland. Two men were on the sprung seat. One was the unmistakable figure of Ed Whelan while the other was a small, squat Mexican with a large sombrero and a rifle across his knee. Ed Whelan drove the rig with skill across the uneven ground. There were two other riders. Both were mounted on small ponies and wearing the obligatory sombreros. They also appeared to be well armed and kept at a distance of some twenty feet behind and to the sides of the rig. Ed Whelan had been careful to provide himself with plenty of protection.

The wagonette drew level with Dave Anders and was pulled to a halt. The big man looked all round as if expecting to see some similar guards hidden among the bushes and rocks. He smiled a little and got down from his perch. His wheezing almost drowned the noise of the springs in the wooden seat. He ignored Dave Anders and went straight to the mule to open the panniers and look at the contents. The rattling of the guns as he checked each one was the only noise disturbing the morning air.

He nodded his head after a while and turned to face the young man who now stood a few feet away.

'We got ourselves a deal,' he said chestily. 'If you throw in the mule as well.'

Dave nodded. He was aware of the three Mexicans, one on the rig and the other two sitting their horses within shooting distance. He was not prepared to argue at this stage.

'You get the mule,' he agreed. 'Now tell me what you know about the folk in Riva Canyon.'

The fat man took a deep breath. 'Not a great deal,' he said. 'Len Forman has sold me things several times. We got us a few good deals since I settled on this side of the border. When he brought them carbines, he told me the weirdest story you ever heard. I didn't believe the fella, but you've backed it up. I reckoned as how he was just coverin' up for somethin' he'd done.'

'What exactly was the story?'

'Well, he rides into Halo Township, so he says, and hears that there's been a gold-strike in Riva Canyon. He decides to go out there and see if there's some miner he can hold up for his poke. But there ain't a soul there when he goes to the canyon. All the gear is lyin' around but there are no men or horses. He couldn't believe his luck. Now, that didn't seem reasonable, but that's what he said.'

He rubbed his hands against the sides of his black coat. His wheezy voice held a note of envy.

'So he loads all the rifles he can carry and makes for the border. We did a deal and then he headed back to see if he could get some more before other folk discovered what had happened.'

'And didn't he have any idea where the miners might have gone?'

Whelan shook his head. 'I don't figure as how he cared. The guns was all he wanted.'

'How did you pay him?'

'Mostly in gold-dust.'

Dave Anders nodded his satisfaction. He now knew where the dead man's gold had originated. He stepped away from the mule and Ed Whelan gestured to one of the riders. The man took the animal's rope to draw it away while his boss felt in his pocket and produced a bundle of money.

Dave took the cash with all the calm he could muster, but his hand trembled slightly as he counted the notes. A gentle breeze caught one of the bills and it fluttered gently to the ground. Dave Anders bent to pick it up and there was a sudden clatter of metal among the pebbles that littered the earth.

Both men looked down to see what had fallen. It was a marshal's badge that had slipped from the lawman's waistcoat pocket.

NINE

The fat man moved with the speed of an angry rattler. His right hand slipped under the flap of his black coat and produced a Colt .44. It was cocked and pointing straight at the lawman before Dave Anders had time to make a move.

A shot cracked the stillness of the air, and before the marshal had even drawn his own gun, Ed Whelan was staggering back and falling to his knees. He was cursing vividly but the blood that poured from his mouth turned the words into a choked gurgle.

The Mexican who still sat on the rig was the first one to do anything. He pulled back both hammers of the shotgun and levelled it at Dave Anders, The marshal fired before the man could pull the triggers and the shot took his enemy high in the chest. The man tumbled backwards from the seat and ended in a dying sprawl that rocked the little wagonette on its springs.

The other two Mexicans were undecided. One turned his horse to flee the scene while the one who had taken the mule hesitated for a moment. By the time he went for his gun, Dave Anders was in full control again. He fired another shot and the man's left shoulder jerked in a spasm of pain as the bullet went home. He turned his horse with a savage thrust of the large spurs and galloped after his fleeing companion. The marshal was left with the mule, the guns, and all the money.

He stood for a moment, undecided and wondering where the shot had come from that had saved his life. A horseman appeared from behind a clump of tall cacti and rode confidently towards him with an old Sharps carbine across his left shoulder.

It was the Indian agent and he greeted the marshal with a wide grin as he laid the gun across his saddle and patted it fondly.

'Haven't made a shot like that in years,' he said cheerfully. 'I told you that Ed Whelan was one mean man. What happened?'

Dave Anders told him and showed the recovered badge and the pile of money that had dropped to the ground and been scattered a little by the breeze.

'Well, I suppose we could claim the reward for him,' the agent said ruefully, 'but you'd have to travel a couple of days with that fat carcass reeking like an angry skunk. I reckon we'll just have to leave him here for the Mexicans to deal with.'

He looked at the money wistfully.

'However,' he murmured, 'these poor Indian folks could use a few dollars for things the government don't provide.'

He raised a quizzical eyebrow and Dave Anders passed him the money without any regrets.

The marshal took his time riding back to Halo Township. He reached the little place in the early evening, and after unsaddling his animals and feeding them, he went down the street to report to the mayor. The first citizen was a worried man. Women were asking where their husbands were. None of the local prospectors had yet returned and people were now really worried about them.

The marshal told all he knew, but at the end of it all, the two men were none the wiser. He stored the pistols in his office and retired there to have a long rest from the wearisome journey.

Nearly two weeks later the first of the prospectors hit town. He rode in on an unsaddled horse, his face grey with fatigue and his whiskers growing into a substantial beard. A crowd gathered round him to help the man stagger uncertainly to the saloon for a long glass of beer. Somebody ran for his wife and she came running to wait outside the swing doors until he had slaked his thirst and emerged to greet her with a hug.

Somebody else had alerted the marshal and the mayor. Both men hurried from their offices to push through the crowd and carry the man off to the privacy of the jailhouse where he was able to sit down in front of the old desk while his wife stood quietly in the background to hear his tale.

Dave Anders poured him a cup of coffee and added some whiskey to it to help the narrative along. The man supped gratefully before starting his story.

'We was workin' away, all normal-like,' he said hoarsely. 'Just gone noon, it was, and I was thinkin' of stoppin' for a bite to eat. Then all of a sudden, these fellas came tearin' at us from both ends of the canyon, hootin' and hollerin' somethin' awful. They fired shots in the air and there weren't a goddam thing we could do about it.'

'Do you know who they were?' the mayor asked anxiously.

'They wore masks,' the man said bleakly, 'and the brands on their horses were covered over with mud. They rounded us up like cattle and took us all to the southern end of Riva Canyon. They had two big wagons there and we was loaded into them.'

He held out the mug for more coffee and Dave Anders obliged. The man gulped the drink noisily.

'We couldn't see much after that and if we tried

lookin' through the canvas, somebody would lash out with a gun barrel. They was mean as hell. I don't know where we was headed for certain, but the shadows on the canvas made me think we was goin' north. That turned out to be right, because after two days, we hit the railroad.'

'Two days!' The mayor almost shouted the words in disgust.

'That's right, Mr. Mayor. Two days of real hard travelling. They fed us from time to time, but we sure as hell moved some distance. They opened up the back of the rigs and we could see that there was a chuck wagon with us, and all our horses were there. But there were no saddles, and all we had were the clothes on our backs.'

He sniffed audibly before continuing.

'Then a train arrived. It weren't no regular train. Just a few cattle trucks is all. They put us in one of the horse-boxes and ran our animals into two more of the trucks. We was locked in good and tight, and off we went.'

'A specially ordered train,' Dave Anders murmured as he glanced at the mayor. 'That needs powerful friends.'

'It means ranchers,' Mayor Penning growled. 'Sam MaCready's brother is a director of the railroad, and Joe Jenkins has an interest in it. They're behind this, Marshal, you can wager on that.'

Dave Anders nodded. 'I'd agree.' He turned to the

96

prospector. 'What happened then?' he asked.

'Well, I reckon as how we must have travelled for the best part of another day, and then, when we was gettin' real hot and thirsty, the train stops. It was mighty dark by then and we're ordered out to stand there like convicts while they covers us with their guns. Then this fella says as how they're lettin' us go free and we can ride our horses back home. But he said as how we'd not get treated so easy if we went back to Riva Canyon. Then they unloaded our animals and left us there. The train went back the way it had come and we just had to try figurin' out where we was and how to get back to Halo Township.'

'And you never recognized any of them?' the mayor asked.

'Not a one, Mr Mayor. I just set off for home, and I reckon as how the others is all followin' on as best they can. It was one long, wearisome journey, I can tell you, and my horse is half-dead after it.'

'Well, you're the first to get here,' the marshal said cheerfully. 'How many do you reckon were in the canyon?'

'Of us? I figure on sixteen from town and about twenty others that we didn't rightly know. Four or five were ranch hands who gave up their jobs with the Double J or the S bar M.'

'I think you'd better stay away from the canyon until all this is sorted out,' the mayor said thoughtfully. 'It's not worth the risk, and the ordinary work of the town is sufferin' by men leavin' their jobs to look for gold.'

The man nodded glumly and got stiffly to his feet.

'I can't argue with that, Mr Mayor,' he said in a dull voice. 'All I want right now is a square meal and a warm bed. I don't plan to go prospectin' again in a hurry.'

'Did you find any gold?' the marshal asked quietly.

The man blinked. 'Never caught sight of anything,' he said in a defeated voice.

When the man had left the office with his wife and a collection of friends and neighbours, Dave Anders poured the mayor a drink. 'Orderin' up a train takes a lot of organizing,' he said as they drank. 'They'd have to use the telegraph.'

The mayor's head jerked up and he nearly spilled the precious liquid.

'Of course! You're right there, Dave. And this is the nearest town with a telegraph office. Maybe you'd better have a word with Walt Griffin.'

'I aim to do that, but he'll probably tell me that telegraph business is sorta private-like. I might have to get a little rough.' He looked hard at the mayor and recieved a sympathetic nod.

'I'll stand by you on that, Dave. Shake the little jackrabbit until his teeth rattle, but find out who sent the message to the railroad company.'

The marshal was entering the telegraph office a few minutes later. It was a quiet place, now lit by two oil-lamps and with the shirt-sleeved operator at his desk in front of the equipment. The man was young and stooped, with prematurely grey hair and a lined face that was pale and thin. He wore silver-rimmed eyeglasses and his scanty hair was cut short and smoothed down with pomade.

He looked up as the lawman closed the door and greeted him with a grin.

'Got a message to send, Marshal?' he asked in a business-like voice. 'The line's free for the present so I can send it off pronto.'

'No, Walt, I haven't got a message. I want to know about one that was sent from here. Somebody ordered up a special train. Tell me all about it.'

The man blinked and went slightly paler. He shifted uneasily on the padded stool.

'Can't do that, Marshal,' he said piously. 'Rules of the company. All messages is confidential. More than my job's worth.'

Walt Griffin could never quite say afterwards what happened next. He was dragged from his seat and somehow ended against the rear wall of the office with the marshal's hand around his neck and gun thrust under his long nose.

'Walt,' Dave Anders said quietly, 'if you don't tell me what I want to know, I am goin' to pistol-whip

99

you all round this room. Now, don't make me get mad at you, and don't try tellin' me the company rules. This concerns the folk of Halo Township and they want this information. If they don't get it, you'll be in real trouble and the company won't help you.'

'I can't tell . . . !'

'If the folk round here know that you ain't helpin' them, they're apt to ride you outa town on a rail. Just like they did to Yankee supporters in the war. All tarred and feathered.'

'I – I don't mean no harm, Marshal, but he threatened me.'

'I'm threatenin' you, Walt, and I'm right here. He ain't. Now, talk, lad. While you still can.'

'It was Lew Jenkins,' the man gasped. 'He came in with a message from his pa. All written down it was. He was orderin' a special train to meet a passel of horses and riders ten miles west of Brihuega Flats. The railroad company queried it but Lew told me to send another message to point out that the McCready family, as well as Joe Jenkins, was orderin' it. We had to wait about half an hour before we got the answer, but they agreed to send the train on the date it was ordered. Them ranchers sure have power, Marshal. Lew Jenkins scared the hell outa me.'

Dave Anders relaxed his grip. He had scared the telegraphist even more than Lew Jenkins had been able to manage. And he had all the information he needed.

TEN

Joe Jenkins got down from his horse and went across to the flowing creek that meandered over the plateau of stunted grassland. He bent to scoop up some of the water in his large grasp and pulled a wry face as he tasted it.

'Look at that,' he snapped angrily as he let the drops fall through his fingers. 'Still as sandy as hell and not fit for sheep, let alone cattle. It should have cleared by now. It's been the best part of a month since we rode off them prospectors.'

His son edged his own horse nearer to the stream.

'They've had enough time to get back, Pa,' he said tentatively.

'You reckon? After the scare we put into them? I doubt it. From what I've heard, they're still gettin' back to town a few at a time. We left the bastards without saddles or guns. They had one long journey home, and I figure on them havin' enough of gold huntin' for a while. No, we gotta take another look

102

at that canyon, lad. There could be new folk pokin'
round there, and we have to deal with them now.'

The youth leaned eagerly forward in the saddle.
'Shall I go, Pa?' he asked.

Joe Jenkins hesitated. He was short-handed
since some of his own men had joined in the gold-
rush.

'You'd better. I can't spare anybody else while
we've got those steers to ready for market. Just see
what's happenin' and let me know. If there are
some fellas diggin' back there, I'll contact Sam
McCready's sons and we'll make up another church
outin' to give 'em a hard time.'

'I'll see to it, Pa.'

'You do that, but don't go killin' folk this time.'

Young Lew set off an hour or so later. He rode
eagerly towards the canyon, armed with his
Winchester, a Colt .44 and an itchy need to prove
himself against anyone who upset his family. His
father was a tough character, a veteran of the war,
and of pioneer stock. Lew wanted to be like him; to
earn his respect.

Riva Canyon looked empty when he reached it.
He rode to the entrance carefully, keeping his horse
on the grassy areas and away from noisy scree that
would herald his arrival. He tethered the animal
behind some trees, took off his spurs, and entered
the place quietly with the Winchester cradled in
his arms.

103

He had gone some fifty yards when he heard something. There were voices ahead round the next bend. He stole forward to peer out between some clumps of mesquite at what was happening on the bank of the creek. There were three men there. He recognized one of them but the other two were Mexican labourers, and they were the ones doing the talking as they panned clumsily in the swiftly flowing water.

The man he recognised was Pete Weldon's son, Nathan. The youth was bending down with a metal pan in his reddened hands. He was swirling the contents with as much ineptitude as the two Mexicans showed. The three clearly did not really know very much about panning for gold.

Lew Jenkins almost smiled at their efforts as he watched. Their horses grazed close by and there were a couple of small tents with a fire lit near one of them. It housed a large enamel coffee-pot that filled the air with the fragrance of its contents.

The watcher hesitated. He could easily kill all three. The Mexicans did not appear to carry guns and Nathan Weldon only had a shotgun lying a few yards away. It would have been so easy but he remembered what his father had told him. He made up his mind and decided to frighten them off instead.

He stepped out from the shelter of the mesquite with the Winchester cocked and levelled. The three workers heard the hammer going back and all froze for a moment before looking up and seeing the determined face of the young rancher as he stood only a few yards away.

'You folks will never learn,' he said, as he approached. 'My pa told you about spoilin' the water, and you still ain't got the sense to let folk live in peace. Now, get the hell outa here before there's more shooting.'

Nathan Weldon was not as timid as he looked. He put down the pan and crossed to where Lew Jenkins stood. The two men were only a couple of yards apart, both about the same build and height.

'We got rights here,' Nathan said bravely. 'My pa's got three claims registered in this canyon and nobody's gonna stop us workin' them. That's the law.'

Lew Jenkins blinked. He had not expected opposition and he waved the gun menacingly in a determined effort to bluster rather than to lose face.

'I'm tellin' you to quit, fella!' he shouted. 'I don't give a damn for no law. You folks is poisonin' this water and my pa's got a livin' to make. Now, get the hell before I starts shooting!'

Nathan Weldon forced a grin. 'I don't figure on you bein' that much of a fool,' he said with all the firmness he could muster. 'The folks round here already know that it was your pa and McCready's sons who scared off the others by shippin' them out like cattle on the railroad. The county sheriff and the town marshal are gettin' a posse together to do somethin' about that. You got enough trouble, fella.'

Lew Jenkins bit his lip angrily. His immature features showed up the uncertainty as the gun wavered restlessly in his hands.

'I ain't backin' down!' he blustered in a loud voice. 'I aim to have you outa this canyon one way or another.'

'Best thing you can do is to go back home,' Nathan told him quietly. 'There's been enough killin' round here.'

Lew Jenkins hesitated. He was thinking of what his father would say, and what his father would do. He was being laughed at by some town lad whose pa was a mortician. He gave a shout that was almost one of despair and pulled the trigger.

Nathan Weldon's mouth opened in sheer surprise. He stood for a moment as though unhurt and then plunged gently forward to the ground. There was a large bloody patch on the upper part of his back where the bullet had emerged. The two Mexicans watched silently while Lew Jenkins stood as if amazed at his own stupidity.

Then he realised that there were witnesses and turned the Winchester towards the two men.

'*Cuidado!*' one of them shouted as he made a dive for the nearest cover.

The other man was already moving. He drew a

short knife from its sheath and flung it at the man with the rifle. It caught Lew Jenkins in the lower body, just above the belt buckle, and buried itself to the hilt.

He let out a yell and dropped the Winchester as he tried to pull out the deadly weapon. The Mexican ran across, picked up the gun, and swung it high above his head. He brought it crashing down on the rancher's skull and Lew Jenkins dropped dead beside the man he had just shot.

The two Mexicans looked at each other, and then began to collect their gear. They tightened the girths on their ponies and headed for somewhere safer on the other side of the border.

ELEVEN

The funeral was over and all the folk of Halo Township had turned out for the melancholy internment of Nathan Weldon. His father had performed his usual duties with the same solemn air he normally displayed, but there was a genuine sorrow that etched the gaunt face of the mortician.

Young Lew Jenkins had been buried out on the Double J ranch alongside other members of that old-established family. Nobody in town bothered to mourn for him. Everybody knew by now that the ranchers had been responsible for organizing the train that took the gold-hunting menfolk into the wilds.

They were all walking away from the burial ground when Joe Jenkins rode into town with his foreman. The rancher was a big man on a large horse and looked neither to right nor left as he headed for the marshal's office and tethered his animal to the rail.

His foreman was a slightly shorter version of the boss; a tough-looking man with wide shoulders and tanned, rugged face that was set in determined lines that boded no good for anybody who crossed him. The two men looked through the window of the jailhouse, discovered it to be empty, and stood uncertainly on the stoop.

At this moment folk came round the corner from the burial ground and began trooping down the main street. Joe Jenkins got some hard looks as they passed him, but he ignored them to await the approach of Dave Anders.

The marshal was walking with the mayor and the two men drew to a halt in front of the rancher and his companion.

'I woulda thought you'd be out chasin' them Mexicans,' the rancher said harshly.

Dave Anders shook his head.

'I got no reason to chase Mexicans,' he said.

The rancher flushed angrily. 'They killed my boy!' he shouted so that all the street could hear. 'Them Mexicans knifed my Lew and shot Nathan Weldon. What sort of lawman is it that skulks in town while folk like that are on the rampage?'

'Them Mexicans killed nobody,' the marshal said in a clear voice that could easily be heard by the gathering crowd, 'except in self-defence.'

'Self-defence! What in hell do you mean? My boy was stabbed and Nathan was shot.'

'With a Winchester.' The marshal's voice was flat. 'And it had the Double J brand on the stock.'

There was a silence while the rancher struggled for something to say. Then Dave Anders went on remorselessly:

'I visited the canyon a few days ago, and all the weapons that Nathan Weldon and those two fellas had, was one shotgun and a couple of knives. Your son went there lookin' for trouble. And he got it.'

'That is one big lie, fella!' the rancher shouted. 'My boy was taken by surprise. They killed him first and then used his gun to shoot Nathan Weldon. That's the truth of it.'

'Now, why should they do that, Mr Jenkins?'

'Why? It's obvious, even to some no-good kid of a town marshal. They was thieves.'

The mayor coughed politely. 'What did they steal?' he asked with deceptive innocence.

'How the hell do I know what they stole? Ask your useless lawman here.'

'They stole nothing,' Dave Anders answered calmly. 'Just packed their bed rolls, took their own horses, and went back home. Your son had fifteen dollars in his pocket and a watch. He also had a valuable Winchester and a .44. Nathan Weldon had five dollars and a tin watch. Then there was the shotgun and the horses. If they'd been thieves, they wouldn't have left things like that behind.'

Pete Weldon had come to join the throng in front

of the jailhouse. His lined, thin face was only enlivened by the gleam in his pale eyes. His right hand rested on an inside pocket of the black frock coat that covered his lank figure.

'That's the truth of it, Marshal,' he said hoarsely. 'Them Mexican fellas was as straight as ramrods. They never would have hurt my boy. Lew Jenkins did the killing, sure as spit, and I reckon his pa sent him there to do it.'

A derringer sprang into sight as he uttered the words and the noise of the hammer clicking back was as loud as a clap of thunder in the now silent street. Joe Jenkins went for his gun at the same time, but staggered back against the jailhouse window as the mortician's shot took him just below the chin. His elbow broke the glass as he slid to the planks with blood streaming down his chest.

The foreman had already drawn his gun and fired a single shot at Lew Weldon. It took the mortician high in the left shoulder and he reeled backwards into the arms of the people behind him.

The mayor scrambled for cover among the tethered horses and the marshal found himself alone in front of the ranch foreman who pointed the re-cocked .45 at him. The crowd were now some twenty feet away and none of them seemed inclined to interfere.

'Put up that gun,' Dave Anders said with a calm he did not feel. 'There's been enough killin' around here. Get your boss's body on his horse and take it back home for burial.'

The man hesitated. His .45 was firmly pointed at the lawman but he now had no employer and the street was full of folk who had no love for the Jenkins family. He nodded his head and placed the Colt back in its holster. With the help of Dave Anders and a couple of other men, he got the body of Joe Jenkins across the saddle of the horse and led the animal slowly out of town.

The doctor had arrived by now, bending over the mortician who was still moaning as he lay on the wooden steps.

'He'll live to bury us all,' the medical man said with grim humour. 'Help me get him to the surgery. And easy now, he ain't the lightweight he looks.'

Several men rushed forward to help the stricken mortician who let out another loud groan as they moved him. His watch fell from his waistcoat and dangled by its chain until someone tucked it safely back into his pocket. Something else had also fallen to the ground and Marshal Anders picked it up as he retrieved the fallen derringer at the same time. He held onto both objects for safety, and it was not until he and the mayor were having a drink in the jailhouse, that he opened the little cotton bag.

It contained about two ounces of gold-dust.

TWELVE

The Golden Globe saloon was quiet that evening. The regulars leaned on the bar drinking their beer while a few card-players were gathered in one corner. The oil-lamps smoked a little and the smell added to the depressing atmosphere of the place.

Phineas Cutler looked round carefully as he entered through the swing doors. He nodded to those he knew and went to join a few of the old-timers at the long counter where the two bartenders were wiping glasses.

Phineas bought more beer for his neighbours and leaned his squat figure against the wooden counter.

'I suppose you'll be goin' back to Riva Canyon, Al?' he quizzed the man on his right. 'Too bad to have to miss out on a good thing and leave Pete Weldon to bag the lot.'

The elderly man shook his head. 'I don't figure to

113

take another ride in a railroad wagon,' he said sourly. 'I'm too old for that sort of thing. I'll leave it to the younger fellas.'

'Joe Jenkins and Sam McCready are dead, and that gun-totin' Lew Jenkins got killed as well. I don't reckon as how there's any danger now. Why should Pete Weldon have it all? He ain't really one of us.'

The man on the other side of the storekeeper decided to join the conversation.

'But look what happened to his son,' he said. 'Even if there is gold there, it don't do much good if you lose your kin findin' it.' Phineas drew the two men closer and lowered his voice:

'Did you see the little cotton bag that fell outa Pete's pocket when he was shot?' he asked. The two men nodded.

'The marshal and the mayor don't want us to know what's goin' on,' Phineas whispered, 'but I reckon as how there was gold in that bag, and that Pete's son and them two Mexicans had panned or dug it out of Riva Canyon. Why else would Pete be so keen to work his claims when the rest of you was spooked off?'

'I never found any gold there,' one of the men said sadly. Phineas Cutler gave a slight chuckle and winked.

'I bought dust and nuggets off various fellas,' he said, 'but I ain't sayin' who got lucky. Folks as dig up gold ain't too keen on other folks knowin' about it. That canyon still has a few surprises if I ain't mistaken.'

Jake Fenton was in the saloon that night. He saw Phineas Cutler but preferred to drink by himself. He nursed his glass of whiskey as he watched the poker game with little interest. He heard the gossip that was going on around him and noticed Phineas talking to the two men at the far end of the bar.

Something was nagging away at the back of Jake's mind, and he looked round the smoky room to see if the man he wanted was there. Old Billy Wilton was leaning on the bar with a glass of beer in his gnarled hand. He looked as if he was trying to make it last as he stared glumly into space.

Billy was unwashed and unshaven. His clothes were old and worn. He stood alone because the old-timer had a smell all his own that nobody else was keen to share. He lived in a small hovel at the edge of town, ekeing out a bare living by doing odd jobs for the more charitable housewives who took pity on him. His sons had gone away years ago to earn their livings in Tucson and the old man had been forgotten, even by his cousin, Phineas Cutler.

Jake Fenton moved quietly down the bar to stand at the old man's side. The smell of unwashed flesh was strong but the storekeeper smiled at his companion.

'Haven't seen you around for a long time, Billy,' he said cheerfully.

'I bin around for them that's interested,' the man replied in his reedy voice.

'Well, I don't come in here for a drink very often. I'm just about ready for another one. Will you join me?'

The rheumy old eyes lit up as Jake Fenton called the barman and ordered more whiskey for himself and another large beer for Billy. 'I've got a little job for you if you've time to spare,' Jake said persuasively. 'There's a job needs doin' round back of the store.

'The old man took the glass in both hands and raised it to his lips. He took a grateful swallow before answering.

'What sorta job?' he asked cautiously.

'That picket fence needs paintin' again. I reckon it'll take a few days. I'd rather you do it than anyone else. You was always a good hand with a paint-brush.'

'I'd like that right fine, Mr Fenton. Right fine. Tomorrow?'

'As soon as you can make it, Billy. My wife's naggin' about it. You know how the ladies are. And that reminds me, I must be makin' for home or she'll think I've run off with one of Ma Gibson's girls. What time do you make it?'

The old man fumbled for a moment towards his

waistcoat pocket and then withdrew his hand with an embarrassed grunt.

'Ain't got my watch on me.'

Jake Fenton looked surprised. 'But you always had that fine silver one that General Van Dorn gave you. You ain't lost it, have you?'

The old man snorted angrily. 'Lost it to my own kin,' he growled. 'That damned Phineas has got it, blast him.'

'How did that happen?'

'I ran up a bill in his store. Times was hard, but I reckoned on gettin' enough work to pay him back. When I couldn't raise the money, he took my watch. He knew what it meant to me, but he still took it.'

Jake Fenton knew that he was on the right track and happily ordered another beer.

'Wasn't there a gold nugget on your watch-chain?' he asked in as casual a voice as he could muster. 'Somethin' around the two ounce mark?'

'Nearer three. Yeah, he got that as well. But it's the watch, Mr Fenton. Not the nugget. That was just a keepsake, you might say, of when I was a wild young fella minin' along the Gila River. But that watch – that was precious.'

'I can guess how you feel about it. Now, listen, Billy. Go to Phineas and tell him that you can raise enough money to redeem the watch. And you want it back.'

The old man looked up, his eyes suddenly hopeful.

'But I ain't got that sort of money,' he protested. 'What are you gettin' at?'

'How much was it?'

'Fifty-three dollars and a few cents. That's a hell of a lot for an old soak like me.'

'I'll supply the money.'

A film of doubt passed across Billy's eyes.

'Why in hell should you be a-doin' that, Mr. Fenton?' he asked suspiciously.

'Have you been payin' any heed to this gold rush in Riva Canyon?'

The old man shook his head. 'Of course I ain't. there's no gold there, ain't been for years. But folks is always hopin' to strike lucky so they keep trying. It's a fool's game and I'm too old to be flim-flammed by it any more. Why is you asking?'

'A little bit of dust seems to have been found there. And one large nugget. Near to three ounces in weight. Phineas bought it from the finder.'

The old man blinked. 'Did he now? Was he there when it was found?'

Jake Fenton nodded. 'Yes,' he said.

There was a long silence between the two men while old Billy finished his beer and started on the fresh glass that stood before him. He wiped his mouth with a slightly shaky hand before looking hard at the other man.

'Seems to me as if you're suggestin' that my

cousin has been saltin' the canyon,' he said in a solemn voice.

'I've been thinkin' along those lines, yes.'

'Wouldn't put it past him. He just ain't nice folk. And I also figure you could put him outa business in this town if that came out.'

Jake Fenton smiled. 'It could profit both of us,' he admitted.

'It could. I'd know that nugget if I saw it again.'

'Well, if you got it back with the watch and we showed it to old Jamie Pullen, that would just about clout the nail on the head.'

'He's the fella what found it?'

'Yes.' Jake Fenton felt in his pocket and produced five silver dollars. 'A little payment in advance,' he said as he tucked them into the old man's smelly waistcoat. 'See you in the morning, Billy.'

Neither man paid any attention to the alert eyes of the other storekeeper. Phineas Cutler watched the conversation between his old cousin and Jake Fenton with a great deal of concern.

He had intended to go home but decided to wait around until Jake Fenton departed. He watched the fat storekeeper leave the saloon before going over to join his elderly relative.

'You seem to be popular tonight, Billy,' he said as he slid a glass of whiskey into the man's eager hand.

'I got me some work,' the old-timer replied guardedly. 'Paintin' fences for Mr Fenton.'

'Is that a fact now? I got some work for you myself. Worth ten dollars cash money.'

Billy swigged back the whiskey and turned a bleary eye on his cousin.

'You ain't a man what's over-generous with money, Phineas,' he said bluntly. 'What's the job, and how dirty is it?'

'Do you recall that about twenty years back, you got yourself in a fight over a woman? Up Tombstone way, it was, if I ain't mistaken. A fella got killed, and he wasn't even carryin' a gun'. If that sheriff had been able to find the killer, he'd sure as hell have been hanged. But you was lucky, Billy, because I was there to help you out.'

'That was twenty years ago,' the old man muttered. 'It's over and done with.'

'Sure, but it was still murder. I saved your life, Billy, and now it's your turn to help me out.'

'How?'

'I want you to go to Riva Canyon tonight. There won't be anybody there and you'll be able to leave a few sprinkles of dust in that creek. You're an old prospector. You'll know the best places to put it. I reckon as how there'll be another rush by morning, and I want them to find a little gold. Just enough to keep them interested. Are you in?'

'Ten dollars? And my watch?'

Phineas Cutler smiled. He had judged his cousin right.

'And your watch,' he agreed. 'But not the nugget. I might need that a while longer.'

He ordered more drinks before asking the really important question.

'What were you and Fenton talkin' about? And don't tell me it was about paintin' a fence.'

The old man grabbed the whiskey glass eagerly.

'Same thing we're talkin' about now,' he said with a grin. 'He noticed I ain't got the nugget no more and he wants to get hold of it.'

'I wouldn't like that, Billy, and if you'd done a deal with him, I'd be mighty annoyed. Betrayin' family ain't a good thing. After all, you gotta live around here, and you are a killer.'

The old-timer swallowed his drink hastily. 'Just give me the dust and I'll go saddle my mule,' he said as he wiped his lips.

He left town an hour later and Phineas Cutler went home a contented man.

THIRTEEN

They began leaving town early the next morning. Phineas had opened his store to meet the demand for food and watched them riding out of Halo Township with a smile on his broad face.

All the gold-seekers were quite convinced that Pete Weldon found dust in the canyon, and some had even called at the house where the wounded man lay, to see how true it was. The marshal was also questioned, and his embarrassed manner was all it needed to tell the men that gold had been located. It was also safe to go back to the canyon now that McCready and the Jenkins men were safely dead and buried.

So they set off in high spirits while the marshal and the mayor fretted at all the new trouble that was likely to arise.

Jake Fenton was also worried. He had expected some action from old Billy, but he seemed to have vanished from the face of the earth. The stout hardware dealer chewed the ends of his luxuriant moustache ragged as he went about his business. He felt betrayed after giving the old man so much money in advance.

Two days later he eventually plucked up enough courage to go round to the little hut that Billy used as a home. It was made of odd planks and roofed with canvas and turf. No other building stood nearby and the small corral adjoined it with its mass of twisted fencing and sparse grass.

The mule was there, looking glumly at the intruder while it nudged an empty water trough as if to point out its need. Jake Fenton knocked on the door of the hut. There was no answer.

He did not want anyone to see him with Billy and only tapped gently while glancing nervously around in case he was observed. He decided to look inside and pushed back the wooden latch. The door slid open noisily as it scraped the ground on its sagging hinges. A stale, bitter smell assailed the nostrils and the stout man coughed as the acrid stench caught his throat. The place was dark, the single window covered with an old sack and the only light coming through the open door.

Jake Fenton could see the old man curled up in bed. A whiskey bottle lay on the earth floor next to his boots and the coarse blanket was drawn close to his scrawny neck. The hardware dealer approached and looked down at him.

Billy Wilton was quite dead.

Three men sat in the jailhouse. The mayor, Jake Fenton, and the marshal. Dave Anders had to supply the whiskey and was looking sadly at the amount his two companions had already consumed.

'I was relyin' on him,' Jake said for the third or fourth time. 'Old Billy was goin' to try and get back that nugget so that I could show it to the man who found it in the canyon. It would have proved that Phineas Cutler salted the creek.'

'To think he's doin' them sort of things,' the mayor said quietly, 'makes me real mad. He ain't a likeable fella but that's a low trick. If folk knew about it, they'd be liable to lynch him. Too many people have died over this gold.'

The marshal reluctantly opened another bottle of whiskey for his guests.

'Let's try and get some sense out of all this,' he suggested. 'Ma Conyers came into town and I went out to the canyon with her. Pete Weldon found gold in the gravel her husband had been pannin' and he bought her claims all legal. Then a decent-sized nugget was found and that really started things moving. Small amounts of dust have been found since. All agreed?'

Jake Fenton nodded. 'Yes, but Phineas put the nugget there when we took the wagons out to sell supplies.'

'But the original dust was found by Pete Weldon and he has another couple of ounces now. Did Phineas do that as well? I don't reckon as how he would have planted the dust that Conyers panned out of the creek. And that's what really started it all.'

'Then maybe Phineas helped things along later,' the mayor suggested.

'I reckon that's it,' Dave Anders agreed.

'We can't prove it without the nugget,' Jake Fenton said ruefully. 'It's a pity old Billy died like that.'

'What did the doc say?' the mayor asked.

The storekeeper shrugged. 'Too old and too drunk was how he put it,' he said. 'Not a bad way to go, I suppose, but it don't help us pin anythin' on Phineas Cutler.'

'You could ask to see the nugget that Phineas bought off the prospector,' Jake Fenton said to the marshal.

'I could,' Dave agreed, 'but he could say that he'd sold it on.'

'There's another thing,' the mayor chipped in. 'That fella who was sellin' guns across the border. He had gold. Did he get that from Riva Canyon, Dave?'

'No, he was paid partly in gold for the rifles. He didn't rob anybody for it. I reckon we just have to sit tight and see what happens next.'

Something happened almost at once. The doctor entered the office, put down his bag on the floor and eyed the whiskey bottle thirstily. He accepted a glass and sipped the drink with relish.

'I needed that,' he said as he took a seat. 'I got some news for you, Marshal. Old Billy was murdered.'

Dave Anders half rose from his chair, but then sat down again. The warm room was silent for a moment while they waited for the doctor to continue. It was the mayor who broke the silence.

'You never noticed that when you were called in,' he said somewhat unkindly.

'I thought he'd died in his sleep, and he was old,' the medical man said defensively. 'It wasn't until I saw the body under a better light that I could tell. That hovel of his isn't the best place in the world for an examination, you know.'

'How was he killed?' the marshal asked.

'Smothered. Somebody just put that filthy pillow over his face while he was lying skunk-drunk.'

'Are you sure about this?' Jake Fenton asked. 'He looked so natural when I saw him. Just like he was took with a bad heart."

The doctor looked a little sheepish. 'Well, with Pete Weldon bein' laid up with that bullet wound,

126

and him havin' no help, I had to lay out the body at the funeral parlour. Pete told me how he goes about these things. He always opens the mouth in case they have gold teeth, so I did just that.'

'He don't miss a trick,' the mayor said with grim admiration.

'He even takes their false ones,' the doctor said. 'He told me that he has a fella in Santa Rosa who buys 'em for a dollar at a time. Anyway, I opens Billy's mouth, and there's a feather stuck in it. Well, that don't seem natural to me. If a fella has a feather in his mouth, he's going to spit it out. So I goes back to the hut and, sure enough, Billy was using a pillow stuffed with goose feathers.

'The sharp ends were pushing their way through the worn cover, and when the pillow was pressed over his face, he must have tried opening his mouth and inhaled one of them. Then I really started examining the body. All the signs were there, in the nose and the eyes. He was killed all right. No doubt of it.'

'How long had he been dead?' the marshal asked.

'Oh, a good twenty-four hours, I reckon. I don't know why anybody should want to kill old Billy, though. He only had a few dollars on him and that bottle of whiskey he'd near finished. At least he died fast and happy. It's more than most of us can hope for.'

Jake Fenton refilled his glass with a trembling hand.

'Phineas was in the saloon when I was talkin' to Billy,' he said shakily. 'He was still there when I left. Maybe the old man said too much. He'd had rather a lot to drink.'

'Or maybe you said too much,' the mayor pointed out.

Dave Anders looked uncertainly from one to the other. He hoped that the mayor would take the lead. The leading citizen had a knowledge of law and was acquainted with all the people concerned, but he sat there as though lost in thought. The marshal realized that it was going to be left to him to make decisions.

'I think I'll have a word with Phineas,' he said firmly. The others seemed to breathe a collective sigh of relief.

'He's mighty handy with a gun,' the mayor said tentatively.

'So am I, but I don't reckon on it comin' to that. Phineas is a cautious man. I spoke to Pete Weldon this mornin' and he tells me that Phineas and his son went up to the canyon the other day with food supplies. It was after his visit that some more gold dust turned up. Pete don't see the connection. He wants to think that he bought some good claims. I figure as how it all started with Ma Conyers. Phineas Cutler just carried on where she left off.'

'Could he have been in it with her?' Jake Fenton asked.

'Could be, but I'm inclined to think he just wanted things to go on. Pete Weldon was taken by Ma Conyers. That's how I see it.'

'But her husband was killed out there,' the mayor protested. 'We all went to his funeral.'

Dave Anders tapped his fingers on the desk-top.

'Could you have that skeleton dug up?' he asked the doctor.

'I reckon so, but what do you expect it to tell you?'

Dave grinned. 'It won't tell me anything,' he admitted, 'but you might notice something odd about it. Pete Weldon didn't do more than bundle it in a casket and get it underground. It's a pity we didn't think of callin' on you at the time.'

'I don't reckon as how I could have done much. I can't cure the ones that still have flesh on them.'

Everybody laughed a little bit uncertainly as though not sure whether the doctor was joking or simply being honest. The medical man got to his feet and picked up the leather bag.

'I'll go have a word with the fellas who do the grave-digging for Pete,' he said. 'They can take the casket to his place and we'll open it there. Don't expect too much, though. A pile of bones ain't exactly a way to prove identity.'

The doctor left them and Dave Anders took the

opportunity of telling the others that he would postpone talking to the foodstore owner until more was known about the whole business. They agreed and reluctantly finished their drinks before leaving the jailhouse.

The wooden casket lay on one of Pete Welland's scrubbed tables. It had been opened and the skeleton was on view to the men who gathered around. The grave-diggers had been dismissed with the price of a few beers and only the mayor, the doctor, Marshal Anders and Jake Fenton were left to peer at the remains.

The casket was a cheap one. The cheapest that Pete Weldon provided for those who had little money to spare. There was not even a shroud and the bones lay in a disjointed heap under the soft light of the oil lamps. Old Billy's body lay on another table in a slightly better box with the lid screwed down.

The doctor had brought along a grubby copy of Quain's textbook on anatomy, as well as his worn leather bag. He put his gold-rimmed glasses on the edge of his nose and looked closely at the remains.

'Well, you could certainly have saved yourselves a load of trouble if you'd let me see this before it was buried,' he said with a chuckle. 'How long was this fella, Bill Conyers, supposed to be dead before you found him?'

'About a week,' the marshal said.

'Well, I'm not pretending to be exactly an expert on skeletal remains, but this one you got here has been in that condition for more than a week. Say, about twenty years or more. It's as yellow as the sand in Riva Canyon. You've been taken, Marshal.'

'Then how the hell did Pete Weldon miss that?' Jake Fenton demanded angrily. 'Surely he had enough experience to know the age of a skeleton.'

'He doesn't usually bury skeletons,' the doctor said drily as he looked at the man over his glasses.

'Then this ain't Ma Conyers' husband?' the mayor asked. The doctor chuckled again.

'Not unless she married a middle-aged woman with rickets,' he said cheerfully.

FOURTEEN

It was nearly midnight when the first group of prospectors returned to town. They rode in noisily, throwing up a haze of dust that glittered in the lights of the saloon. There were angry shouts from them, and Dave Anders, who had dozed off in his chair after a large supper, woke with a start.

He went to the window to look out and saw half a dozen or so horsemen rowdily grouped in the middle of the street shouting somebody's name in hoarse voices. He strapped on his Colt, took a shotgun from the rack, and went out to see what was happening.

Their voices suddenly stilled when they saw him approach, and they seemed to wait for someone to take the lead when the lawman stopped in front of them and asked what all the noise was about. One of them swung his horse round until the animal's head was only a couple of feet away from Dave Anders.

'We're after old Billy Wilton,' the rider said in a

loud voice. 'He's been saltin' Riva Canyon.'

Phil Hackman was the speaker. A heavy drinker, he was a man who hardly worked to support his large family. He was quarrelsome and eager to take the lead in any troublemaking. His reddish face and slightly greying hair were covered in dust, but even in the darkness of the street, his pale blue eyes seemed bright and hostile.

'How do you know that?' the marshal asked calmly.

'We seen him comin' from the canyon,' one of the other men said with a sudden burst of courage. 'He was drunk enough to be fallin' off his mule. Real drunk he was, Marshal, but we didn't pay no heed at the time.'

'That's right,' said Phil Hackman, 'and when we got there, some of the fellas started findin' gold flakes in their pans. It seemed a good sign until Bobbie here picked up a watch from the creek. It was the one that Billy always boasted was give him by some general during the war. His boot-marks were all over the place and his mule had been there and left fresh droppings. He'd been salting that creek all along, I reckon. There ain't no gold there but what Billy Wilton planted.'

'And why should Billy do that?'

The men looked at each other but none of them had the answer. It was big Phil Hackman who finally spoke.

'That's what we aim to find out!' he shouted amid a roar of approval.

'Well, he won't be tellin' you,' the marshal said as he stared the man down. 'Old Billy is dead. Somebody killed him during the night.'

The men sat looking slightly bewildered for a moment and the marshal felt himself in command of the situation.

'I suggest you all go home and have some rest,' he said quietly. 'And it might be a good idea to go back to your jobs instead of looking for gold that don't exist.'

He turned to walk back to the jailhouse, hoping to have calmed things down, but Phil Hackman was not yet finished. He had his position as self-appointed leader to think about.

'You seem to know more than you're telling, Marshal,' he challenged. 'What's going on around here that we folks don't know about?'

'Just go home, Phil,' Dave Anders told him firmly. 'The mayor and the councilmen are workin' on it, and we'll have the answers in a few days. In the meantime, we don't want no trouble in town, so don't go causin' any. I wouldn't take kindly to it.'

Phil Hackman's dusty brow was furrowed as he thought out the situation. He looked towards the saloon and then at Phineas Cutler's closed food store. There were lights in the rooms above and Dave Anders could see how his mind was working.

'I've told you to go home, Phil,' he ordered bleakly. 'I don't aim to have a jailhouse full of folk what go jumpin' to the wrong conclusions.'

'We was fooled, Marshal!' the man cried as he tried to hold his restless horse. 'We was all workin' our guts out on a salted creek. Old Billy was Phineas Cutler's cousin, and that vittal-sellin' rogue sent him to scatter some dust around the place. We've just been workin' to make money for Cutler. I reckon that fella's on for a hanging. What say, fellas?'

There was a growl of agreement and the little group of horsemen began to move towards the food-store. Dave Anders reached out to try and grab the reins of Phil Hackman's mount but the man swung it round and the marshal was pushed backwards. He caught his heel against the wooden steps of the jailhouse and fell on the planking. By the time he scrambled to his feet, the men were outside Phineas Cutler's building and dismounting in a noisy group.

Anders ran down the street after them and was just in time to see the crashing of the door as it was booted in to shatter the glass panels and wrench the hinges from the woodwork.

They were inside before he reached the scene and pushed his way through the horses. Other people were gathering now, and out of the corner of his eye, the marshal could see the stout figure of the mayor running up the street followed by Jake Fenton and the doctor. Men had come out of the saloon and a light went on in the preacher's house.

Dave Anders and the mayor ran up the steps and were about to enter the store when two shots shattered the air. The flashes lit up the darkened interior as cries of rage or pain filled the street. A man staggered out through the doorway, bumping into the mayor and nearly knocking him over. It was Phil Hackman with the right side of his chest torn away by a shotgun blast. He swayed towards the middle of the main street to collapse in an untidy heap.

'Quit that shooting!' Dave Anders shouted as another man scrambled from the building. He too had shotgun wounds in his chest and face but did not seem as badly injured. One of the windows had shattered and the lawman found himself treading on broken glass, as he edged towards the dark interior with his shotgun cocked for use.

'I'm comin' in!' he yelled. 'Put your guns aside.'

The place smelt of burnt powder, which had killed the scents that usually filled the well-stocked building. Somebody scraped a vesta, and in the flickering light, Dave could see a man lying on the floor and another two crouching for safety behind sacks of provisions. A fourth man stood against a wall, holding a damaged arm that was dripping blood on to the plank flooring.

It was Phineas Cutler's son, who was applying a light to one of the oil-lamps. The golden glow shone across the scene of devastation to show his father still holding the shotgun ready for any more trouble.

'They broke in, Marshal!' he shouted angrily. 'Near frightened my wife to death, they did. I never did see such drunk behaviour in all my days. I don't know what the hell this town's comin' to.'

'They're not drunks, Phineas,' the lawman said as he took the hot barrel of the gun from the man's hand and laid it on the counter. 'They're just angry folk who think you've been saltin' Riva Canyon with gold dust.'

The storekeeper's face went taut. He glanced briefly at his son as though passing on a warning. Then he tried to compose an expression of complete innocence.

'Well, them's right foolish words, Marshal,' he blustered. 'Why in Hades should I do a stupid thing like that?'

'To make money perhaps,' the lawman suggested. 'I think you'd better come across to my office. Me and the mayor have got a few questions to ask.'

'And why in hell should I go to your office like a common criminal? These fellas were goin' to rob my store.'

'Phineas,' the marshal explained patiently, 'these

fellas were goin' to do no such thing. They was simply goin' to lynch you from the grain-store loadin' beam.'

The man's mouth fell open as he tried to search for words. His son had lit two more lamps and the doctor was using one of them to render treatment to the wounded men. Other folk were crowding into the doorway, enjoying the best bit of excitement they had experienced all week.

'Lynch me!' Phineas got the words out at last.

'That's right, and they was only the first lot. There's still other fellas on their way from Riva Canyon, and one shotgun ain't gonna stop all of them. It might be as well if you was in my office until things quieten down. I can't protect you if you're loose on the street.'

'Perhaps – perhaps you're right. I'll come at once. But what about my family'?'

'Nobody's gonna harm them, Phineas. It's just you they're after.'

The defeated man glanced round the store before walking reluctantly across the street followed by the marshal and the mayor. People looked at the little procession with keen interest. They did not quite know what was happening but Phineas Cutler was clearly in trouble with the law, and nobody particularly liked him.

In the warmth of the jailhouse, Dave Anders poured out coffee, and, it being an official occasion, did not provide the mayor with a whiskey bottle. The three men sat round the desk with the large enamel mugs in their hands. Phineas Cutler's drink was spilling as his fingers shook. He raised the mug to his lips and tried to look unconcerned. His hands told a different story.

'About what happened back there in the store,' he said. 'I was in the right of it. I fired in self-defence.'

'I'm not interested in what happened at the store,' the marshal assured him. 'They was lookin' for trouble, and if you hadn't started shooting, I'd probably have had to do it.'

The lawman put down his steaming mug.

'I'm more interested in the death of old Billy,' he said. 'He didn't go natural. He was murdered.'

The storekeeper's hot coffee trembled like a rising tide and some of it fell into his lap to make him squirm uneasily. 'Murdered?' he repeated.

'Yes. Smothered with his pillow. He hasn't had that silver watch of his for the past year or so. You took it off him in payment of a debt. But he had it with him when he went up to Riva Canyon to salt the creek. And he was so skunk-drunk that he dropped it there. I reckon you killed him, Phineas.'

The man jumped to his feet. His face was ashen but there was a stubborn and dangerous look about him. The mayor pushed his own chair further back from the desk as though afraid of being attacked.

'You can't go around accusin' me of things like that!' the storekeeper shouted angrily. 'I got some standin' in this town and old Billy was kin. A man don't go round murderin' his own kin. And why should I do it anyway? What reason could I have?'

'Because what them fellas said back there was true and you was saltin' the creek. From the very beginning.'

Phineas hesitated for a moment and then finally sat down again. 'You've got no proof,' he said as firmly as he could. 'Nobody ain't gonna say as I harmed old Billy.'

'We'll leave it for the visitin' judge and a jury to decide, Phineas,' the marshal said as he stood up and took down the cell keys from their hook on the wall.

'You ain't lockin' me up!' The man jumped up again and his chair fell over.

'You're safer here than turned loose on the town. If you do get hanged, at least it'll be all nice and legal.'

Before the lawman could unlock the cell door, Phineas Cutler had drawn a Colt .44 from under his coat. The clicking of the hammer and the frightened yelp of the mayor made Dave Anders turn round from what he was doing.

'That's a fool move, Phineas,' he warned. 'How far do you think you'll get?'

'Far enough. I reckon my boy knows his duty and

140

has a horse waitin' for me out there. I'll take my chance at goin' south, away from this no-good town. Now, open that cell and take yourself and the fat man in there where you can't do no harm. Lock the door and throw the key out to me. And no tricks, because I've got nothin' to lose.'

The marshal did what he was told and the mayor needed no urging to scuttle into the small cell while the lawman turned the key and threw the bunch onto the floor in front of Phineas Cutler.

'Now your gun,' the storekeeper said sharply, 'and your itsy-bitsy derringer, Mr Mayor. Throw them out here and do it careful-like.'

The two men obeyed and their captor went over to the window and looked out. The street was surprisingly quiet. The doctor had ordered the removal of the dead and wounded, the crowd had got bored at nothing further happening, and the saloon had decided to stay open a little later to accommodate them.

A horse stood at the corner of a side-street, held by young Will Cutler. The youth was looking anxiously at the jailhouse, and saw his father wave to him. He brought the animal round to the back door and waited for the storekeeper to emerge.

'I've put some food and money in the saddlebag, Pa,' he said tautly. 'You shouldn't have done what you did, but Ma says we gotta stand by you.'

'Your Ma's a wise woman, son,' the fugitive

answered as he looked round the side lane. 'Run the store if they'll let you. If not, load everythin' up and follow me to your Aunt Ettie's place. Now, get off the street before anybody sees what's goin' on.'

He flung his heavy frame into the saddle and headed for the southern edge of town. Shouts could be heard from inside the jailhouse, but the people who were awake and still away from their own homes were having a last drink and gossip in the saloon.

FIFTEEN

The story was all around town by early morning. There was anger, but also a certain wry amusement at how the mayor and the marshal had been locked up while their victim escaped. More prospectors had come back to Halo Township, weary and furious at knowing that they had been hoaxed by one of their own neighbours.

The food store was closed and young Will Cutler was sitting in the marshal's office confronted by Dave Anders, the mayor, and several members of the town council. He had spent the night in the cells, as much for his own safety as any other reason. It had been decided not to bring him before the judge. The lad was not considered very bright and everyone in town was of the pioneering stock that believed in the solidarity of family life and its obligations. There was even a sneaking admiration for how he had helped his father.

He had eaten breakfast and was now sipping

coffee while the others were listening to the marshal interrogating him. The youth kept insisting that he did not know where his father might have fled, and nothing they could say would move him on that point.

The mayor took the lead when Dave Anders got tired of asking questions.

'Look, Will,' he said kindly, 'your pa killed old Billy and swindled a lot of people around here. We gotta bring him before a court or we'll not be doin' our duty to the folk who rely on us. Do you understand that?'

The youth nodded stolidly. 'Sure do, Mr Mayor, and I don't like what Pa did for one minute. I helped him get away, and I reckon as how that was my duty, like Ma said. But that's all I do for him. He's on his own from now on, and I ain't aimin' to help him no more.'

'That's fair enough, lad,' the mayor agreed, 'but where will he be heading?'

'With all respect, Mr Mayor, I don't reckon as how I can tell you that,' the lad answered in a low voice. 'It wouldn't be right.'

'Where did he get the skeleton?' the marshal asked as he poured more coffee for those who wanted it.

'Skeleton!' The youth looked as if the question had no meaning.

'The one we found in Riva Canyon that was

144

supposed to be the body of Bill Conyers.'

'I don't know of no skeleton, Marshal. He never said anythin' to me of a skeleton.'

'He had to have someone to help him, Will. Did you go along to dig it up from a burial ground?'

The youth looked offended. 'No, of course I didn't,' he protested. 'That would be indecent. My Ma wouldn't let me do a thing like that. We're Christian folk.'

'Then who would have helped him? There had to be someone else.'

'I don't know. I just don't know, Marshal, and that's a fact.'

Jake Fenton leaned forward in his chair and it creaked under his weight. 'Who was the woman?' he asked urgently.

'What woman?'

'Landsakes, lad! You know all too well what woman we're talkin' about,' the mayor interposed. 'Your pa had a woman workin' with him. She came into town as Ma Conyers and started this whole business. Who the hell was she?'

The lad shook his head in apparent bewilderment. His face was sullen as he stared at the floor.

Jake Fenton suddenly clicked his fingers and let out a yell of triumph.

'Of course!' he crowed. 'Phineas has a sister out at Santa Coloma. Ettie Burke. She'll be the one who helped him. Her and her husband were in charge of the ferry there, and she took over when he got himself shot for trying to swindle some timber traders. That's where Phineas will be headin' for right now.'

The men did not need to question young Will any more. The look on his face told them that Jake Fenton had guessed right.

Dave Anders looked out over the wide sweep of the valley. The river ran through the centre like a wide thread of silver under the glaring heat of the sun. The grass was dry up on the slopes but more lush as the ground levelled off towards the sandy shores. There were cattle there, their brands dark against the pale hides as they stood silently up to their knees in the sweet grass or wandered to the edge of the water to drink.

It was a long journey to the ferry-crossing at Santa Coloma. The marshal had a mule with him to carry supplies for the six days that the trip would take there and back. He was not optimistic but the effort had to be made. He was half a day or more behind Phineas Cutler and had little hope of sighting the man on the trail. And if the marshal was seen approaching the ferry, the storekeeper could easily cross the river to end up in the safety of Mexico.

The trouble was that he had to travel along the

bank of the river and there was no way that he could approach the area of the little pueblo without being seen from a great distance. The land was too flat to hide a rider unless he went in by night. That was what he intended to do if things turned out well. But if he sighted Phineas Cutler, it would create problems. The man only had to turn in the saddle to be equally aware of his pursuer. If that happened, the lawman would have the disadvantage of being hampered by a mule while the other rider could make off at whatever speed his horse was still capable of achieving.

As the marshal stared out now over the wide valley, there was no human being in sight. He seemed to be the only person in a vast wilderness. It was his second day on the trail and he led his animals down to the water for a drink while he made a meal for himself before resting through the heat of the afternoon.

The day was uneventful, but as the light was beginning to fade and the sun disappeared into low cloud, Dave Anders spotted a thin streak of smoke some distance away. It was a small camp-fire being lit, way out to the west and with the white plume going straight up in the still air. He halted and got down from his horse. If he tried to move nearer the man might be alerted and the chase would be over. He decided to make camp for the night, but without a fire until the last of the daylight had gone.

He could not travel over unknown country in the darkness. The moon would be hidden by the clouds and the ground was too uneven to risk damage to horse or mule.

He took a cold meal of bread and cheese and then lay down under the patchy sky to get some sleep. The chill of the night woke him after a couple of hours and he lit a small fire in the shelter of a clump of bushes. Hot coffee worked wonders and Dave Anders sat warming himself as he listened to the sounds of darkness and the steady rustle of the long grass.

It was the horse that alerted him to something beyond the glow of the fire. His mount had been standing quietly near the mule, its head lowered and its breathing heavy. Then it suddenly looked up and across the marshal's head towards some wind-bowed bushes that lay some twenty yards over to the west. They were quivering slightly and shaking a fine drift of dust from the leaves.

Dave Anders reached out for his .44 but decided instead to roll over towards his saddle-bags where the shotgun lay next to the Winchester. He grabbed the scatter-gun, cocked both hammers, and let fly at the low bushes.

Acrid-smelling smoke blew back in his face as a scream of pain came from the darkness. The marshal jumped to his feet, threw the shotgun aside and drew the Colt. He ran towards the bushes, tripping over clumps of grass as he moved

148

round behind them to find a man writhing in agony on the ground.

It was Phineas Cutler. He still clutched a Winchester and tried to aim it at the lawman. Dave Anders kicked it from his grasp and knelt down at the side of the man he had been pursuing.

'You're hurt bad, Phineas,' he said bluntly, 'and there ain't no point in tryin' to hide it from you.'

The man nodded agreement. Both charges from the shotgun had caught him in the upper body, and although fired at some range and having been partly deflected by foliage, they had damaged him badly. He rolled over to lie on his back and looked up calmly at the lawman. 'Then you win all along the line, Marshal,' he admitted. A slight trickle of blood came from his mouth as he tried to grin. 'Don't let them blame my wife and boy. He didn't tell you where I was heading, did he?'

The question was a plea for reassurance as much as anything and Dave Anders was quick to comfort him.

'No,' he said. 'It was Jake Fenton. He recalled that you had a sister in Santa Coloma.'

The man chuckled. 'He would,' he said almost cheerfully. 'Never did like me, that Jake Fenton. He was always jealous of the business I did. But I got too greedy. That was my trouble. Are you figurin' on takin' me back home?'

'No, it's too far. I could take you to your sister's

place.'

'Yeah, I'd not mind bein' buried there. It's only another ten miles, but look out for Ettie. She don't like lawmen and she fires a mean scatter-gun.'

Dave Anders smiled in the darkness. 'I'll watch out,' he promised. 'How did you know I was following you?'

The man chuckled again but his voice seemed to have a slight gurgle. 'My folks settled these parts,' he wheezed. 'I know this borderland like I know my own store. I saw you at dusk. You was movin' care-ful-like, but there was still daylight behind you and the sky over there was still clear. So I lit a fire, and then doubled back and waited until. . . .'

He started coughing and raised a hand to his mouth.

'You waited until I settled down,' the lawman prompted.

'That's right. I didn't aim to go back for a hang-ing. Not for the sake of a drunken coyote like Billy. He made a mess of things and threatened to tell the folks if I didn't give him back the gold nugget as well as the watch.'

'So you and your sister planned it all.'

The man tried to sit up but a sudden gush of blood set him coughing desperately. The marshal cradled him in his arms until the spasm was over. When he spoke to the man again, there was no answer. Phineas Cutler was dead.

SIXTEEN

Dave Anders did not set off for Santa Coloma until late the next morning. He had wasted time finding where the dead man had left his mount, and then had the problem of hoisting the heavy body across the saddle. With the mule and the extra horse in tow, his progress was slow through the hot day and it was getting dark by the time he saw the distant buildings of the little pueblo. The township fronted the border river where heavy cables marked the path of the ferry across the deep, fast-flowing water.

All the huts were of faded adobe, scoured by wind and the occasional shower of rain. There were not more than twenty buildings in the place, with no real street other than a broad patch of trodden earth that led down to the river bank.

A few dogs ran out yelping to greet the visitor but nobody emerged to see who was doing their pueblo the honour of a visit. Dave Anders looked round for some sign of a jailhouse or church. He wanted to find some place that had official status, but other than a cantina and a food store, there was nothing.

He decided to go into the cantina and entered the dimly lit place to be greeted by a strong smell of grease and human sweat. It was a small room with a bar at one end made of three barrels topped by a couple of stained planks. There were a few tables, occupied by drinkers who seemed to be mostly Mexican. The bar-tender was a short man, also from the south, and had a flat, unmoving face and took no interest in customers as long as they paid for their drinks.

There were only two oil-lamps lighting up the place. One was suspended from the dark ceiling while the other was in front of a mirror that hung behind the bar. The marshal ordered a beer and looked in trepidation as the man wiped a glass on his dirty apron before filling it with some cloudy liquid that seemed to be all froth.

'Have you got a burial place in town?' Dave Anders asked as he sipped the drink cautiously.

The man nodded blankly and his glance travelled beyond the lawman to somebody who was sitting at a table watching the newcomer. The man was a tall fellow of middle age with several days growth of beard and one eye partly closed by a scar.

He rose to his feet and came across to stand

beside the marshal. His good eye took in the badge and he motioned the barman to leave them.

'You got someone to bury?' he asked in a grating voice.

'Yeah. There's a fella outside who's beginnin' to smell a bit,' Dave Anders answered.

The man went across to the dirty window and looked out at the three animals that were tethered to the rail. He came back rubbing his chin thoughtfully.

'You got money to pay for him?' he asked.

'That's his horse he's laid across. I reckon it'll cover the cost of a burial.'

'And the saddle.' The man's voice was businesslike. 'I'll need the saddle.'

'And the saddle.'

'Then we got a deal, Marshal. What name shall I put up for him?'

'Phineas Cutler. From Halo Township.'

The man let out a thin hiss through his scanty teeth at mention of the name. He peered hard at the lawman as if doubting what he had heard.

'Are you tellin' me that you got Ettie Burke's brother lyin' across that saddle?' he asked in wonder.

'I reckon so. He was comin' here to hole up with her. Is she in town?'

The man nodded vigorously. 'She sure as hell is, and she ain't gonna be one mite pleased at this sort of news. She's one fightin' woman, Marshal, and right now, I reckon she's mad at the whole world.'

Dave Anders grinned. 'And what's the world done to her?' he asked.

'She runs the ferry, and the army came along a few weeks ago and closed it down,' he said. 'Ettie was sore as hell. She took a shotgun to the soldier boys and they was lucky to stay in one piece. That made 'em real mad though, so they put a hole in the ferry and now she's got no way of earnin' a living. It's sunk at its moorIngs and she's one wild woman.'

'Why the hell close down the ferry? It's the only crossing for miles.'

'It's this revolution business them Mexicans is playin' about with. They need guns, and all sorts of fellas was usin' Ettie's boat to manage a little tradin' across the border. Ettie was doin' right well out of it, but now she's holed up in her cabin. She's shootin' mad at anyone wearin' a uniform or a lawman's badge, and she's nigh on certain to start firin' as soon as somebody like you hoves in sight. Just stay away from her, Marshal. Leave Phineas to me and get yo'self outa town before she hears about his death. No point in meetin' up with Ettie.'

'I have to arrest her,' Dave Anders said firmly. 'Her and Phineas have been makin' trouble for a lotta folk who have died because of them. She's goin' back for trial, whether she's mad at the world or not. Is there a lawman in town?'

'No, we can't pay for one. Now, let's have one more drink and I'll take Phineas and his horse off your hands and dig a nice grave for him first thing in the morning.'

Dave Anders ordered more beer. It tasted better than it looked and the two men drank silently before going out to the animals to complete their deal. After watching the tall mortician depart with the dead body, the marshal led his own animals out of the little pueblo to camp further up the river where the air was cleaner.

The morning was bright, without a trace of the low cloud that had obscured the night sky. He rode back to the pueblo, raising a dust from the reddish soil beneath the hoofs of his two animals. He passed the closed cantina and rode down the slope to the ferry. His companion of the evening before had told him where to find Ettie Burke. Her adobe cabin with its red-tiled roof was on the edge of the water, only a few yards from the ferry boat that was partially sunk near the bank.

It was more a broad platform than any other sort of vessel. It sagged on its cables as the river flowed over it and broken pieces of tree branches caught up along its sides.

He was nervous. Arresting a woman was some-thing he had only had to do on two occasions. He was now far away from home with a long journey ahead of him. It was bad enough with a male prisoner, but with a female, he hated to think of the problem.

And yet he was anxious to meet up with the woman who had made a fool of him and started all the killing. He unholstered his shotgun in case she decided to make a fight of it.

The adobe hut looked clean and well kept. The windows bore yellow net curtains and the door was painted a bright blue. It was firmly closed and there was no sign of life. Dave Anders got down off his horse, tethered it with the mule to a nearby fence, and approached the building cautiously. He held the shotgun in both hands, the hammers cocked, ready for use.

What happened took Anders completely by surprise. There was a shattering of glass as one of the little windows flew in jagged pieces to reveal a scatter-gun that blasted both barrels almost simultaneously. The charge of shot would have cut the lawman to ribbons had he not dropped to the ground at the noise of the breaking window. His horse let out a loud neigh of pain as pellets tore into its flank while the mule collapsed in a writhing mass on the earth. It kicked for a few seconds and then lay still.

Dave jumped to his feet, ran at the door, and heaved his weight against it. It gave way and he found himself in a small room thick with the smell of the discharged shotgun. He stumbled over a thick wool rug and nearly dropped the weapon from his grasp. The room seemed empty for a moment but he suddenly became conscious that something was moving in the shadows.

The woman had been behind the wrecked door. She was swinging the discharged shotgun above her head to bring it down on the intruder.

The marshal rolled over on his side and pulled the trigger instinctively. The flash and violence of the explosion seemed to burst the eardrums in the confines of the little room. He heard her body fall but his own eyes were smarting from the smoke that blew back at him from the open door.

When he stood up and blinked the tears away, the body of Ettie Burke could be picked out quite easily in the dimness of the cabin. He had nearly blown her head off.

SEVENTEEN

Dave Anders was quite a hero when he returned to Halo Township. The crisis was over. Everybody knew that Riva Canyon had been salted by Phineas Cutler and his sister, and all the men were back at their normal jobs. Jake Fenton and a few other traders had lost some business, but even they felt a sense of relief that things were safe again.

While they were quietly celebrating the end of the killings, a middle-aged couple were driving their rig towards a little town called Allington up on the Gila River.

They had already dumped the skeleton in a small gorge and left a few grains of gold in the pan ready to be found. The woman had the reins while her husband smoked his pipe and examined the newly lodged claims that they had just registered at the assay office.

'Got everything straight, Ma?' he asked affectionately.

'As straight as ever, Pa,' she replied as she steered the bay gelding. 'But I sometimes wonder if we're doin' the right thing.'

He looked at her in suprise. 'Don't think that way, honey,' he urged. 'It's just takin' money from rich rubes fool enough to fall for a good flim-flam. We're only puttin' a few dollars aside for our old age.'

'I guess so. After all, nobody gets hurt.'